To Katie

THE RIVER HOUSE

Dedication

This book is dedicated to all persons, living or dead, that violence has affected. Crime thrillers have become one of the most desired genres. We read the books. We watch the television shows. We've become fascinated with the minds of serial killers, but their victims and families don't give a shit about their mind. They just want their loved one back. If their life wasn't taken, their mental peace was. To anyone who has been the victim of a bully, an assailant, murderer or any other type of abuser, please know that I've written these pages with you in mind, not a fascination with the weak-minded bastards who have taken a piece of you away.

Suspect   1

Monster   14

Terminated   26

Midway   35

Come on In   47

Tick-Tock   59

Dr. Cooper   70

Reservation   80

Coward   95

Advisory   105

Behavioral Specialist   115

Slipped Away   127

Unexpected Clue   138

Attraction   149

Want to Play a Game?   162

The Wall   173

Prisoner   185

Time's Up   195

The Last Victim   205

Chapter 1

Suspect

Sunday, April 15, 5:00 a.m. (Three months ago)

Todd Merritt, Mount Placid's Chief of Police, sat in his recliner. His black robe covered his checkered boxers and white T-shirt. The only light in the living room was the glow of the modest flat screen on the floor stand against the wall in the corner. The sound was indistinct. A cheery anchorman spewed the morning's headlines.

Good morning and happy Sunday to all of our viewers. I'm Chris Morris and the time now is 5:00 a.m. Hope everyone in the local area and surrounding counties has an umbrella and rain boots. You know what they say about April showers.

Police are investigating a double homicide on the far East side this morning. We have very little details, but our field correspondent is on location as we collect more details.

The fourth annual Puppy Pace 5k is next Saturday. There's still time to register to run. This is the largest 5k event in the state. All proceeds benefit local animal shelters. Bring your canine to the 5k.

These and more headlines are coming up on Mount Placid News; but first, let's talk about the rain amounts over the next three days. Meteorologist, Charlie Wannamaker has more. Charlie?

Yeah, Chris. You're right about April showers but this is going to be extreme. Our average rainfall for the entire month of April is just under five inches. Get this; we're getting over three inches by Tuesday morning. We're still about an hour away from the rain beginning and it will start light, but once it reaches Mount Placid, this system is going to hover over us for a while. There will be periods of heavy downfalls, so grab your umbrella on your way to church this morning. Tomorrow's early rush hour is going to be a mess, I'll tell you; it will not be a nice day. Threats include heavy rain, flash flooding, pooling on the edges of the roads and interstates and the worst; for those of you in the low areas along the banks of the river, we expect the river to rise thirteen feet. That is not an ideal scenario for one-story homes.

Todd sipped from a steaming cup of black coffee, shook his head and muttered, "It's not a good scenario for young ladies either, Charlie." He picked up his cell phone and called the station.

"Police department, is this an emergency?"

He spoke quietly, "Paula, it's Todd, good morning."

"Good morning, Chief. What can I do for you?"

"I need Sergeant Spicer please."

"Hmm, I just saw him a minute ago. Hang on, I'll go find him. I don't think he's at his desk."

Chief Merritt stood from his recliner and walked to his bedroom at the end of the hallway. He heard Sergeant Spicer's voice through the phone, "I'll get it in my office. Go ahead and put him through."

He heard Paula's distant response, "Okay." She put the phone back to her mouth. "Chief?"

Merritt spoke softly so he wouldn't wake his wife, Karen, "Yeah?"

"I'll put you through now."

The phone rang once. Todd walked out of his bedroom as Spicer answered, "Hey Chief, it's Spicer. What's up?"

"Is your door closed?"

"Hang on."

He heard the phone clang on the desk, then the muffled sound of the door closing. A few seconds later, Spicer said, "It is now; what's up?"

"Did you see the forecast?"

"Yeah, we're going to be busy for a few days."

"Yeah, we are. My biggest concern is that river. It's going to rise. They're saying thirteen feet."

Spicer was silent and Merritt continued, "You know what this means?"

He sighed and fretted, "Yeah, Chief—I do."

"Look, I want you to take one officer off patrol from each district. I want them rotating by the River House. They don't need to go all the way to the end of the lane, but I want presence there. One of two things is going to happen. Either he doesn't kill again because of our visibility or we'll be close enough to get him this time. I want this fucker caught."

"Chief, I'm not saying I disagree; but you know it doesn't happen every time the river rises."

"I know. That's what makes him so damn good at it. Keep your distance. That's my direction to all patrols. Keep your distance. I want to be close enough to move in, but far enough away to tempt this bastard. I'll be in by 6:30."

"Alright Chief. Anything else?"

Chief Merritt asked, "What's the situation with the double homicide?"

"Same shit. Late night party. Some young dude got drunk and shot two of his buddies in a fight."

"We have him, right?"

"Yeah, we got him. He's all tore up about what he did. Apparently, the three of them were really close once upon a time. Now he's getting sober, so he's not as tough as he was when we first got there. Oh, you know him. It was the Brunner kid."

"Shit. He's been in and out of trouble for six years. I think we had him in cuffs when he was twelve. Maybe this will wake his ass up a bit."

"He's not a minor anymore."

"No, he's not—poor dumb fucker. Look, I'm going to let you go so I can get ready. I'll see you in a bit."

"See you in a while, Chief."

"Hey! Do me a favor. Put the river murders file on my desk, will ya?"

"Sure thing, Boss."

"Later," Todd said, before he ended the phone call.

He walked towards the double-pane window to the right of the TV and pulled the curtains open. He sipped his coffee and looked out from his two-story house on a hill. The end of his long driveway met the road that few traveled, unless there was an event at the park directly across the street. Activities at the amphitheater were to start on the first Friday in May. The distinct silhouette of the concert venue was the only structure that blocked his view of the one-hundred-foot-wide Placid River. The yellow lights from buildings high on the opposite bank reflected off the river in long lines and waved lightly with the right-to-left current. Most of the structures on those banks were higher and safe from the rising river, unlike the ones two miles downstream or a mile upstream. The downstream housing was in a poorer part of town, and the upstream residents were wealthy.

Todd entered the station at 6:24. His uniform was pressed, his boots shined, and every silver insignia on his uniform was perfectly placed, as always. Paula greeted him, but he only cast a hint of a smile and a lazy wave, then walked straight towards his office. The files he requested were on his desk. He closed his door, sat in his executive chair and stared at the closed folder that was at least four inches thick. He sighed as he tapped it with his forefinger, then put his hands on the arms of the chair and leaned back. There was a knock on his office window, which got his attention. Sergeant Spicer pointed to the folder, nodded his head, waved, then moved on.

Todd didn't *need* to look at the pictures again. They were burned into his memory, but every time it rained, he requested the file and flipped through its contents. He *had* to be missing something. He sighed again, leaned forward and opened the folder.

Victim #1: Claire Barnett. Recovered from the river on April 15, 2013, the second day of rainfall. The first photos were at the bend in the river at the amphitheater. She was face-down, and her blonde hair spread through the water, like steam wafting from a hot biscuit that was torn in half, then dissipated. Chief remembered the events clearly. Her torso bobbed with the waves of the light current.

The next few photos were of crews pulling her out of the water. Todd recalled that he himself set up a blue flexible wall around Claire's body to hide her from bystanders. The rest of the photos were close-ups of different parts of her body. From her feet to her stomach, there were no visible cuts or lacerations. Her shins had bruises from when she kicked her murderer as she fought for her life. There were bruises on the sides of her neck and across her shoulders, and a solid ring around her neck where something strangled her. It was something thick enough to cause a distinct bruise, but thinner than a rope, roughly the size of a thin dog's lead. Her eyes were glazed over and opaque.

He turned all the photographs upside-down on the left side of the folder, then looked at the cause of death on the coroner's report, homicidal drowning.

He flipped back to the photo that showed the bruises on the sides of her neck and cupped his hand towards the photo. The left side of her neck, as Todd viewed the photo, had a single bruise. The right side had four bruises. He rotated his right hand while he turned the photograph back and forth with his left hand and noticed how the bruises matched where fingers would have grabbed the front of her neck to force her head under water, so he could watch her lights go out when she stopped struggling.

Victim #2: Marie McDonough was also recovered from the river at the bend by the amphitheater. Other than having dark hair, the events and statistics were very similar to what was in Claire's file. Her body also surfaced after two days of steady rain.

There were nine victims; all found similar to Claire and Marie. Five were found after two days of rain. Three of them were recovered after three days of rain, and one was recovered from the river after heavy rainfall for twenty-four hours.

The river flowed from North to South, and there were thirty-eight houses that stretched the banks of the river to the North of the amphitheater. Twenty-seven of them were large homes, owned by wealthy people. The farthest one, that borders the grounds of the nature preserve, was a mile and a quarter North of the outdoor venue. Average income families occupied the other eleven. During each case, Todd's team questioned the residents of every home. None of which has ever seen a body floating down the river. His best conclusion was the killer drowned the victims so that they sank to the bottom, then carried downstream by the strong current under the surface. The right bend in the river at the amphitheater was sharp, and there was a support wall that started at the edge of the structure's foundation. To the North of the support wall, there was

7

a natural river bank. That's where the bodies surfaced. Bits of flesh swirled around at the sharpest part of the bend.

Chief Merritt could have stared at that folder all day. Some days, he did. For as many times as he flipped through the contents of the file, he was no closer to securing evidence to support what he already knew. The young, single anesthesiologist in the modern multi-level home at the end of Rivers Edge Lane, was the one committing the heinous acts. Dr. Brent Cooper purchased three lots at the end of the lane when the previous residents died. Betty in August. That was six years ago, then her husband, Herb, in January a year and a half later. Two members of their extended family cleaned up the property the best they could, between January and the end of June. When they put the house on the market, it sold within a week. Dr. Cooper scheduled closing on the house on a Saturday. Powerful storms passed on Friday morning. Lightning struck a transformer at the edge of the property, which started a blaze in a large, detached garage. The fire was hot enough to melt most of the siding on the main house, some twenty feet away from the garage, and blew a softball-sized hole in the electrical box in the second lot. The house on the third lot was condemned. Herb demolished part of it before he passed. When the executor's realtor contacted Dr. Cooper to inform him of the damage to the property, he requested the current caretakers collect quotes for repairs and turn them over to him, then delayed the closing for three weeks.

It never made sense why a wealthy young man would purchase three properties that were nearly destroyed by the fire along the Placid River. Not to most people, anyway. It made perfect sense to Todd, and he was determined to get the evidence to convict him.

Just before he closed the file, he jotted a note on a small, yellow pad of paper:

Claire - recovered from the river two months after Mr.

Cooper completed the construction of his new home.

Home designer and contractor are people he knew

from Washington State, where he lived before moving

to Mount Placid.

When he finished writing, he tore the small sheet of paper off the pad and stuck it to the cover sheet inside the file. He touched the photograph of Claire from when she was alive. Somehow, to rub his thumb across her image made her more human; more real than just a case of a dead girl pulled from the Placid River.

He reached for his desk phone and pushed a button, called out, "Spicer," then let it go.

"Yeah, Chief."

"Everybody available right now?"

"For the most part, yes. All the patrols are pretty quiet right now. Adams wrote out a speeding ticket, but that was probably an hour ago."

Todd looked at the wall clock in his office and thought, *Damn. I had no idea I sat here that long already.* He looked around his waist, then reached to his shoulder where his walkie talkie usually was. He leaned towards the phone and pushed the button again, "Will you bring me your walkie?"

"Sure chief, I'll be right in."

Sergeant Spicer came into Todd's office and handed him his two-way radio. "All personnel, this is Chief Merritt, I need you all to listen up."

Each officer listened closely for Chief's message. The ones on patrol turned up the volume on their walkies to hear over the sound of the wipers on delay. Two of them, that weren't in their cars, were partners that just finished breakfast. Both of them turned their radios down in the restaurant and leaned their ears close to their shoulders to hear.

"If you haven't seen the forecast, it's supposed to rain for the next three days. You all know what that means."

Before he continued, he thought of his transmission through police scanners all across Mount Placid.

"Everybody, change to internal, 10-18."

"10-18" wasn't the internal channel. It was the code to let everyone know this was urgent. He waited for a full minute and continued, "If I'm right—and I think I am—we'll be recovering a body from the river on Tuesday or Wednesday. Unless—"

The partners put cash on the table, left the restaurant and waved at their waitress on the way out.

Todd paused and took a deep breath. "Unless we get this—" He considered the hefty fine if he said "fucker" on the radio. "*guy* before he does it again. I want a patrol around the clock at the end of Rivers Edge Lane. I want you close enough to move in, but far enough away so that we're not obvious. When it's time to move in, go 40, 10-4?"

Everyone knew he meant a silent run. They would move in on the River House without lights or sirens. He turned to Spicer when he let go of the button on the side of the radio, "I want Matthews in a boat, yes?"

"Yes, Sir."

Matthews was their only undercover officer who had been on the force for 3 years, and no one in that little town suspected he was anything more than a friendly citizen. He had a long beard and was as fit as a man could be. As far as the public knew, he was self-employed and made a living out of woodworking from the shop in his detached garage.

Chief continued on the radio, "I also want one patrol around the hospital on Wednesdays. That's when the suspect is there. And I want one more around his office, next to the hospital. Questions?"

After a brief pause, the radio beeped with responses, "I'll take his office building."

"182, you copy?"

Officer Nelson replied, "182, I copy."

"Okay, great. Thank you."

"Chief, it's Baker. I'll take the hospital on Wednesday. The other days, I'll be on Rivers Edge."

"Thanks, Baker."

"Anybody else?" he asked.

Silence fell across the radio, other than the rumbling brown noise that came from the speaker.

"Alright, if anyone else wants to volunteer a shift, let me know; otherwise, I'll assign the rest." He paused again. "10-4?"

They each responded over each other, "10-4, Chief."

Sergeant Spicer asked, "Chief, you want me to—"

Without looking at Spicer, Todd interrupted with, "You're dismissed. If there's nothing else, I need my office."

"Yes Sir," he said when he stood and left the office.

Todd watched like an eagle until Spicer was out of sight, then fully extended his keyboard drawer, removed it from the guides and set it on his desk. It tipped forward. He looked up again to see if anyone was coming. The mouse that was to the right of the keyboard slid forward and onto his desk. He glanced out his doorway again and along the frosted window to look for silhouettes. With his palm up, he reached towards the middle of the bottom of the desk, but still couldn't find it. He pulled his hand back out and moved his chair away, then bent over to look. There it was. The reach was uncomfortable, and he slid his palm along the underside of his desk again. He paused when he felt it, then stood up to close his door that Spicer left open and locked it. When he sat back at his desk, he looked along the windows to his office one more time. He sat back down, reached towards the middle of his desk and pulled the business card away. The clear tape that secured it to the desk came with it. With only a glance, he sat it on top of his desk, behind the tilted keyboard drawer. It was a white card with black numbers on it, but no name. He pulled his cell phone from his hip and dialed the number.

His eyes darted from side to side as the line rang three times. When the call connected, no one greeted him, which is exactly what he expected, then softly whispered, "Suspect."

A digitized voice came from the other party. "Yes."

"Mount Placid, TN. Anesthesiologist. Dr. Brent Cooper. The end of Rivers Edge Lane. We have recovered nine victims from the river, near the amphitheater." He described the rest of the details, then waited for a response.

Neither party spoke for a full minute, but Todd knew he shouldn't make a sound.

"When?"

Todd tapped his desk and hesitated when he saw the silhouette of a person walking by the frosted glass of his office. When it was clear, he said, "Now."

The call disconnected, and he returned the mysterious business card to the underside of his desk. Exactly fifteen minutes later, he received a notification on his phone through a text message with a link. Under the link was a message, DO NOT REPLY. He touched the link with his forefinger and a contract opened. He scrolled as he read every word. When he reached the bottom of the contract, he completed the digital signature on the last page, then touched the small rectangle with the word, "Submit."

Dots flashed on the bottom of the message window until another message appeared.

> *This call never happened. The contract*
> *doesn't exist. Stay the fuck out of my*
> *way. I'll notify you when it's time.*

As he looked at his phone, another notification appeared on his screen that read, MESSAGE THREAD DELETED.

Chapter 2

Monster

Moments Later (*John Wolfe*)

I was in the grocery store when my satellite phone rang. I pressed it to my ear firmly and turned the volume down. Without saying a word, the call connected, and a digitized voice said, "Leave now, John."

I left my overflowing cart in the middle of the aisle and walked out the glass double doors, then jogged through the rain. My car was five spaces down the first row to my right as I left the store. The coordinates came across my phone just as I closed my door. *What the hell? This must be a mistake.* But Sam didn't make mistakes. I looked at the coordinates again and shook my head, thinking I must have read them wrong, but this wasn't new to me. I knew how to read coordinates. I mumbled aloud, "Shit, that's on the North Side."

The assignment I received that day was about three miles from my house in Mount Placid, Tennessee. By my best estimation, it was close to the river, possibly right *on* the river. It had to be at the North edge of town. Mount Placid wasn't all that big.

I accessed the podcast list, but nothing new uploaded. There's usually more time between my departure and when I have time to download the podcast with the details of my new assignment. For that matter, there's usually more distance, too. I refreshed the screen twice with the same result before the podcast finally downloaded on the third try. I backed out and went to the last parking space in the lot, which was a fairly secluded place against a line of trees. There were at least a dozen spaces between me and the next car. When I settled, I put in my Ear Pods and listened.

White male, forty-two years old, one hundred sixty pounds, brown hair, anesthesiologist. Body count: nine, over four and a half years. Sexual predator who targets women between the ages of eighteen and twenty-six. Owns an elaborate River House which gives him easy access to dispose of the bodies. There's a bend at the river near an amphitheater. I assume you're familiar with it. That's where the bodies are surfacing.

I listened to the rest of the details and was a little surprised, but not entirely shocked. It surprised me because things like that happened in the big bad world beyond the boundaries of Mount Placid. Places far away from my home. I wasn't entirely shocked, because this world is full of evil assholes who aren't quarantined to special 'asshole reservations.' For a moment, I thought to myself, *how is this shit happening right here in Mount Placid*? Nothing ever happened in Mount Placid other than too damn many festivals and, from May to October, sunset concerts at the amphitheater.

It was futile to question the reasoning. I pulled out of my parking spot, turned on my wipers and drove towards Rivers Edge Lane. If I was a smoker, I would have reached the destination before I finished my cigarette.

The narrow dirt road made it nearly impossible to observe any of the homes incognito. River Road curved along the Placid and the entrance to Rivers Edge wasn't obvious. It dropped at a steep angle. If anyone was coming out of Rivers Edge, it was impossible for another to go in until the entrance was clear. The last thing I needed was to sit with my turn signal on, in my POV (personally owned vehicle), waiting for the rich fucker to come out. There were only fourteen houses along Rivers Edge Lane. Correction: make that twelve, since Dr. Cooper moved in and demolished two of the structures at the end. The road was pitted and difficult to navigate. An SUV couldn't go over six or seven miles per hour. Even *that* would jolt the driver around. The Department of Public Works did nothing to improve Rivers Edge Lane. It was a flood plain. Every time the river rose, the current would damage the road anyway, so they stopped tending to it years ago; long before I moved there after selling the house I lived in with Penny and Katie. In addition, there was no way I would take my vehicle to an assignment, no matter the distance from my home. I had to ditch my own and get a rental before I would consider going down the lane.

Mount Placid was little enough to be small, but big enough that nobody gave a shit. You know those places that a person drives along the road and sees someone walking, but knows right away they weren't from that town? Yeah, it's not like that. If anyone saw a stranger walking along the road, the only reason they'd care is because the driver had to swerve towards the double yellow line, and that was typically partnered with a blowing horn and, "Get off the fucking road!"

I continued past the entrance to Rivers Edge and navigated the winding road slowly so I could look for places to hide in the woods between River Road, that I was driving on, and the houses that belonged to the residents of Rivers Edge. The widest part of the woods wasn't more than a hundred and fifty yards, and it was April, for Christ's sake. The trees had leaves, but they weren't full yet and the underbrush offered little cover. There was only one place to access the River House. There was a raised area between a sharp bend in the river and the woods along Rivers Edge Lane. Beyond the berm was an apartment complex. It was the only place I could consider using as an initial access point.

River Road turned ninety degrees to the right at the apartments and ran perpendicular to the river after that. Just as I reached the sharp turn, I had a thought, so I turned fast into the lot for the River Road Apartments. Fuck it; no one knew my vehicle. I had never been there before, and the rain was falling heavy enough that my wipers were steady on and didn't fart every time they swiped the windshield. Additionally, it was Sunday morning, and few people were out, anyway. I drove through the complex with a three-level building of apartments to my left and my right; neither of which were on the river. When

I reached the end, I turned behind the left building and started back the opposite direction with another three-story building to my right. That one was right *on* the bank of the river. As I drove South, I noticed a few empty parking spaces. The ones that would be of greatest benefit were towards the end of the building, near the woods, and right across from the one-way access to exit the complex. I stopped the car and paused for a moment, then looked at the apartment windows around me. No one was looking out, as far as I could see. With both hands resting on the steering wheel, I looked at the woods in front of me. Dr. Cooper's house was a few hundred yards away from that spot. If I could find a place to park in the apartment complex, I could access the woods from there. But what if I couldn't? What if someone saw me get out of the vehicle? In all cases, I would have to abort the mission. Once a person sees a grown man get out of a vehicle and walk into the woods in the rain, they're going to wonder why the hell a grown man just got out of his vehicle and walked into the woods in the rain. People's curiosity is not my friend. Curious people fuck things up, and that's not okay.

Although it sucked, I had "Plan A." I turned left around the South edge of the middle building to reach the exit and turned left onto River Road to continue where I left off. There were more apartment complexes and two large neighborhoods before I reached the stop sign three quarters of a mile away. One neighborhood, Placid Lake Hills, was gated. Placid Lake, as a name, was deceiving. It was a man-made lake in the middle of the housing edition that cried out for a lawsuit filed by a young woman whose child could wander off into the so-called lake. There wasn't a retention fence. *Could be an option*, I considered. It still sucked, but it was an okay "Plan B."

18

I drove on to a nearby car rental, then pulled back out of the parking lot immediately. *They know me.* I had rented a car from them a few years prior. Sure, it was possible they turned all of their employees since I was there last, but it wasn't worth the risk.

"This is quickly becoming a pain in my ass," I said out loud. My mind raced as I tried to consider options to observe the Anesthesiologist without being seen. Every thought I had led to a high potential of a foiled assignment; every thought but one.

The West bank of the river had thicker woods and fewer structures. I wasn't familiar with the streets on the West bank. I had only driven along the road on that side a few times. Best I could remember, the road was further away from the river than River Road was.

I turned North until I reached one road that connects to the West bank with a bridge and turned left. There were still few other cars, so I slowed and considered the layout of Mount Placid. I was a mile and a half upstream from the River House and looked around for pull offs or access roads that led into the woods to my left. When I reached West River Boulevard, I turned left to go South and closer to Dr. Cooper's house. The road was hilly with a few tight turns. The rain and the thick cloud cover made it seem darker than usual. My headlights glared off a sagging set of reflective rectangles on a chain on the opposite side of the road. The chain across the access was far enough off the boulevard that my car fit with only a few feet behind me. The access was unimproved. I imagined how muddy it would get if the meteorologists report I heard that morning was accurate. Charlie Wannamaker's forecast called for rain through Tuesday. He expected the river to rise thirteen feet. I was still

North of the center of town, so the banks were much higher than they were to the South. Those poor bastards were going to have a hell of a mess to clean up by the time the river receded back to a normal level late in the week. The access road continued into the woods and was level, as far as I could see. I popped the release for my trunk, got out of my car hunched over to not get *completely* soaked, and pulled a tire iron out of the trunk. I peered to the North and South on the boulevard. When I confirmed no one was coming, I jogged to the end of the chain and raised the iron over my head. Just before I swung it down to break it free from the post, I noticed the bolt snap that connected the chain to the ring on the post. I relaxed the tire iron to my left side, disconnected the chain, then tossed it past the post on the opposite side. After I tossed the tire iron onto the floorboard of the back seat, I hurried into the driver's seat and closed the door. There were napkins in my console that I collected to wipe my face, then eased along the muddy path into the woods. When I approached the riverbank, I slowed. Dr. Cooper's house was visible at a Southeast angle from my position.

There wasn't activity around the perimeter of the house. A floating dock swayed lightly with the current and extended twenty-five feet at a steep angle into the river, so that as the river rose, the dock would rise with it. It had a course covering that spanned the length so that a person wouldn't slip when the dock or their feet are wet. It wasn't strange that the dock was empty. After all, it was only mid-April and, although rare, Mount Placid has had snow or accumulating ice into the beginning of May. The dock led to a concrete pad with an outdoor water spigot. The pad looked to be just wide enough for a single vehicle. Remember, this dude is a doctor. I'm not talking about it being wide enough for one of those stupid fucking smart cars. Best I could tell, the pad was wide enough for a Corvette, or Lamborghini with plenty of room to walk around. A wall with two windows separated the concrete pad from, I guessed, a three-car garage, entered from the South at the end of River Edge Lane. To the North of the garage was a multi-level deck with a grill on the second platform and, on the upper level, a large hot tub. The deck was built with thick support posts. As far as I could tell, there were no doors under the decking that led to the interior of the house, but it was difficult to see details. It was raining harder and there were a hundred feet of water between me and the River House. Based on the complex structure of the decking—hell, I guess I have no idea what was under that deck.

The second story of the home had few windows on the back. Based on the spacing, it was likely the level with bedrooms. There were two that faced West towards the river and five that faced North. The third floor had a lot of windows and many of them had no coverings. I always wondered why rich people left their windows uncovered. It made little sense. They had the nicest things, so I guess they wanted to show them off to the rest of the world. If they knew what I knew about people, in general, they wouldn't only cover their windows, they might not have any windows at all. The combination of the angle from which I was looking, the hundred feet of pouring rain between me and the house and the unusually dark sky, I couldn't see through the windows of the house.

I looked to my left along the Western bank of the river, then into the river itself. There wasn't a place that I could easily cross. The river wouldn't start rising significantly until late that night or into the early morning. The rain to the North of Mount Placid is what would fill the riverbanks I stood next to. I looked to my right again. Two hundred yards away was the first house on the Western bank. The widow, Mrs. Fields lived in that house. Last summer, her husband died peacefully in his bed. She held his hand as he passed.

Now, I don't know everyone in Mount Placid. Shit, I didn't know twenty people in that little town, but everyone knew about Mrs. Fields, and anyone who lived there, including me, would do anything for that kind little old woman. It's just how it was.

Without a way to cross from the West bank and nowhere to hide nearby, I had no choice but to come back under the cover of night, try to get some cameras set up inside and outside the River House, then monitor them through my app or, in person from the very spot I stood that day. Drenched throughout, I returned to my car, and went to a different car rental place.

"Of course," I said out loud when I pulled up to the building. They were closed. It was Sunday and if anyone in that town was out on a Sunday, it was at one of the three churches. If you weren't Catholic, Christian or Baptist, you had to worship at home or go to another town. In Mount Placid, churches and local farmer's markets were the only doors open on Sundays. With the rain, the farmer's markets were likely closed that day, too.

The circumstances were against me, so I decided it was best to go home so I could properly prepare for the assignment. My job is not one that you'll find on a list of top places to work. It won't be on lists at all. My job is to use the information I receive in the podcast, then monitor the suspect. When I see the perpetrator conducting the same activity as described in the communication, I carry out my job. My job, at its core, is to terminate the suspect without the red tape of the judicial system. Somebody in the Mount Placid Police Department is confident that the man who owns the house I watched on the banks of the Placid River, is the one who has murdered the young girls that have surfaced at the amphitheater. The reason I'm involved is because their evidence is circumstantial, and in our "fair" judicial system, there's not enough proof against him, and the murders will continue. Ironically, my job is to take life, so that lives can be saved. Do I feel reconciled because I can justify killing a man? No. I, too, will be judged one day, and it sure as fuck won't be by anyone who reads these pages. If that's the reason you're reading this, close the book, or turn off the device, but take your judgmental ass somewhere else. I'm a guilty man, but I can look at the guy in the mirror and smile because I'm afraid of no man, including myself—but my judgement day? *That* scares the shit out of me.

I spend little time at home, so my house is modest. When I met with a realtor to purchase this place, my only requirement was that it had to be secluded. It's a farmhouse in the woods on the far East edge of town. It's two miles beyond the town proper, but I still have a Mount Placid address and utilities. The first improvement I made when I moved here permanently was removed the mailbox and established a P.O. Box in town. I only get my mail after hours, so I don't cross anyone's path. With no mailbox, the little dirt path to reach my house is nearly impossible to identify as a driveway. In the years I've lived here, I've had one vehicle come down my drive. It was a police car. When I walked out with a rifle aimed, he announced his purpose with a deep voice.

"Hey, put the gun down. A couple of kids are missing. I'm just looking at options and noticed the gravel drive. Had no idea it was a residence."

I lowered my rifle and welcomed him to search. He got out of his car with his hands out to his sides. He was over six feet tall.

When he got into the house, he said, "I've never been back here," and looked around the small entryway and kitchen.

"Not much to see, I'm afraid," I responded.

He turned and looked towards the door, "You don't have a mailbox."

"No, I don't. Not at my house, anyway."

"What if there's an emergency? We may not get to you timely."

I clicked the weapon to safe and said, "I don't expect I'd need you for anything," then leaned the muzzle into the corner.

"What about a medical emergency?"

"Then I'll give the 911 operator the coordinates. Anything else you'd like to see?"

He smiled and said, "No, I guess not." He offered his hand as a greeting. "My name is Sean Carter. Probably won't see me around much though. I'm moving my family to Indianapolis next month."

I shook his hand, "Good luck to you, then. I used to live there myself."

"You did? Hmm, what a small world. I have an opportunity there. More chances for promotion in a big city. It's not about the promotion, though. I don't really care about positions. We do what's needed, regardless of our title." He looked around again and asked, "You don't happen to know anybody on the force up there, do you?"

"Just one, I guess. A detective—Fuller is his name. He's a good guy. Helped me and my wife—my ex-wife, a lot when—when we needed him."

He placed his hat to his chest and smiled. "That's good to hear. Sounds like I'll be in good hands."

I nodded my head, then walked towards the front door as an invitation for him to leave.

He put his cover onto his head and said, "I'm sorry, I didn't catch your name."

I smiled and replied, "I didn't give it. Name is Floyd—Roger Floyd."

He turned as he walked through my front door and said, "It's good to meet you, Mr. Floyd. I won't be here for long, but as long as I am—if you need anything at all, you're welcome to ask for me."

"Thanks Officer Carter."

Not one vehicle has been down my driveway since, other than my own.

The rain fell heavily on my roof, which created white noise. Although it was still morning, it made me tired. I had an assignment that night, right there in my very own Mount Placid. A murderer. An abductor of young girls. A monster. A monster that deserved whatever was coming to him—and I was prepared to deliver.

Chapter 3

Terminated

With rain gear, some snacks, and my AR-15, I set out at nightfall to the River House. It was pouring when I left my home. Using my POV was a risk, but the message I got from Sam was urgent. "Leave now, John," it said. I'd figure out a rental car in the morning but couldn't wait until morning to act on the lead. It was Sunday night. The bastard was probably home. I didn't know the level of the river, but based on the heavy downpour, I estimated it wouldn't take long for it to rise quickly. It was 10:55 when I set out to the River Road Apartments near the River House. Just as I approached the entrance, I changed my mind to go to a different destination. I was in the apartment complex parking lot earlier in the day. If anyone saw me, it was likely they blew off a stranger's vehicle driving through the complex. If that same vehicle returned late at night, they wouldn't blow it off as a coincidence.

I crept along River Road and glanced to my right as frequently as possible to catch a glimpse of Dr. Cooper's house through the woods. Rivers Edge Lane was dark. The only lights along the broken road were from the residents' porch lights and the sporadic glow of yellowed light through nicotine-stained curtains; none of which came from the River House.

I considered driving onto Rivers Edge. My vehicle was quiet, but the quiet car was no match for the sound of rocks popping from the edge of a tire, then whizzing through the air only to meet a sudden stop with a thud on a wooden porch. Worse, was the distant sound of tires on the wet unimproved road splashing through the inevitable large puddles that littered the road. My options, even under the cover of night, were limited. When I reached the entrance to a row of duplex homes, across from the lane, I turned around and drove towards Placid Lake Hills to implement Plan B. As I drove towards the community, I visualized the next twenty minutes as prediction of my actions.

I pulled into a parking spot, donned full rain gear, opened the trunk to retrieve my AR-15 with its powerful scope, and walked towards the River House along the edge of River Road.

"Plan B really sucks," I muttered while I shook my head, then continued to a flat area off to the right, across from the entrance to the River Road Apartments.

I put all of my rain gear on before I got out of the car. Just as I opened the door, I released the hood and turned on my hazards. When I lifted the hood open, I walked away from the car with nothing more than a .45 on my hip under the black waterproof top. The sound of the rain beating on my hood was loud. I crossed the street and started down a wooded hill, carefully landing each step on the top edge of a tree so I wouldn't slide down the forty-foot embankment. A narrow flow of water greeted my water boots at the bottom of the, typically, dry hill. The water was rising. I crossed easily and walked to my left in a wide approach to the front of Dr. Cooper's house. It had a flat roof and stucco walls like you would see in hurricane regions. The dominant color of the house was light gray with midnight blue trim and a lot of windows facing the woods. The deck that I saw from the West bank wrapped around the house. As I got closer, I confirmed there weren't lights on in the house. That could mean one of two things. Either he was home and asleep or he was working a night shift. The risk level was undetermined, so I erred on the side of caution and kept my distance around the perimeter of the property. My primary focus was on the corners around the eaves to identify any cameras the doctor had mounted for surveillance. I could barely make out tiny dark spots on every corner of the structure. Cameras. A lot of them.

I crouched down, pulled my raincoat over my head and unlocked my phone underneath. After I swiped the screen to the right twice, I found the app I needed. It identified Wi-Fi connections within a large radius, with the closest ones listed at the top. The first one was a random combination of letters and numbers. The second was cleverly called, "FBI Surveillance Van." The third one listed was "b_cooper." I touched the Wi-Fi to connect, and the app showed the usual.

CONNECTION UNDETECTED

I selected the three dots to access the menu and then viewed the other devices connected to the Wi-Fi.

home_PC

work_laptop

livingroom_TV

Apple_TV

security_system

master_bedroom_blue-ray

living_room_blue-ray

room_2_blue-ray

room_2_television

There were many more listed, but I didn't need to look at all of them. When I touched on security_system, a message showed on my phone: CONNECTING.

After a minute, I had access to all the cameras he installed inside the River House. The first eight cameras offered views of the outside of his house. The cameras were listed in groups; perimeter, first_floor, second_floor, and third_floor. All of them had night vision. As far as I could tell, every corner of his house was visible remotely. Camera 8 was pointing directly at me. I waved my arm and saw the same on my phone's screen with a half-second delay, then moved behind a bigger tree.

I looked at every camera on every floor. There was no sign of Dr. Cooper in any of his common rooms. I spent the next two hours crouched under my raincoat and viewed each camera to develop a mental floor plan.

The first floor showed the garage that had a short, wide car under a gray tarp; possibly a Ferrari or Lamborghini. The second bay had a blacked-out Toyota Tacoma on a straight axle and big tires with a black cloth cover over the bed. The last bay was empty.

Just inside the garage was a game room with a couple arcade games, a pool table, a dart board, and a fancy octagon-shaped table for playing cards. Even with the night vision, the last camera was hard to see, but appeared to have a full bar with a mirrored wall behind it.

The second floor was the main living area with a large kitchen and living room. There was a small bar towards the back of the house. When I switched back and forth between that camera and a few of the outdoor cameras, I could see a sliding glass door led to the deck outside. Next to the glass door was a split wall that hinged in the middle. The bottom had a dark wood top, and the upper part could swing open for when he entertained guests on the deck. The swinging door allowed access to the outside where he could serve drinks on the dark wood top.

Beyond the common area was a hallway with several rooms, including his Master Bedroom. That was the only bedroom with a camera. His bed was on a pedestal. The ceiling had a wooden design with recessed lighting and a mirror in the middle. There was a sitting area and closets the size of my living room. Every room had access to the deck outside.

The third floor was very open. There were floor-to-ceiling windows all around. One end had exercise equipment. The other end had a large wall screen with ten movie theater seats in it. There were six leather reclining theater chairs in a row that were curved around four others in front of them. In the middle of the front wall, there was a sliding door to access the deck. He accessed the back deck through French doors to the right of smaller kitchen.

I stretched my neck and put my phone on the belt clip. The rain had lightened some. It was still steady, but not a heavy downpour, like it had been earlier. Very few cars traveled along River Road high above me to my right and no one came down Rivers Edge Lane.

I returned to my car, closed the hood and turned off the hazards. Just as I put the car in gear, a police car pulled up behind me with the lights on. He walked up to the window, and I lowered it.

"Everything okay tonight, sir?" he asked.

"Yeah, sure is. I ran out of gas, but I'm okay now."

"Oh, man. Not a nice night to get stranded. You have a good night now."

"I will, Officer. You do the same."

When he got into his car, I pulled away and went home.

Monday morning, I drove to get a rental car and returned to the West Bank off the boulevard. The chain was still disconnected from my throwing it open the previous morning. The river was raging. There was no activity from the River House for several hours. I pulled up the app to view Dr. Cooper's security system, but he still wasn't there. I looked at the first camera that showed the garage. The far-left bay, looking towards the bay doors, had the car with the cover on it. The Tacoma was in the middle one, which was the same as the day before. Everything was the same except the last bay. A bright yellow Z06 Corvette.

All three vehicles were in the garage. I looked at the second-floor cameras. There was mail on the counter that I didn't see the night before, but otherwise, it was empty. He wasn't there. I checked his bedroom. The bed was made perfectly. I checked the third floor, the game room, and the bar. He wasn't there. It was 10:40 a.m. I looked away from my phone and through binoculars I had around my neck. There wasn't movement on the first or second floors.

31

There was a cover over the third-floor deck. Dr. Cooper sat at a round table sipping coffee with flannel pjs and a thick robe. He had a newspaper spread open and crossed his left leg over his right. Lightning flashed. Thunder exploded into the air and the rain fell harder. Dr. Cooper lowered his newspaper and looked out at the woods and the river. Soon after, he went inside. He didn't act strangely. Only watched television and moved around the house normally. He cooked microwave meals a couple times and took a shower at 9:00 p.m.

He left in the Tacoma at 9:45 that night. I got into my rental and sped South on the Boulevard, then East on River Road to follow him, but never caught up until I was at his office building near the hospital. He parked his truck near the front of the building in a reserved parking space. I watched him through the first-floor window with the binoculars. While at his desk, he pulled paper files, then typed into the computer. There was an occasional visitor, but nothing notable. He appeared to give instructions to a young male visitor, then laughed playfully with a female visitor.

Tuesday was similar, but he didn't go into work that day. He spent most of the day on his porch and then went inside to cook a boxed microwave meal. I stayed there until he went to bed at 11:45 p.m. and occasionally monitored him from home after I linked the two Wi-Fi connections. He woke up once around 2:15 a.m. to pee, then returned to his bed. That's around the time it stopped raining.

I left home and was at the pull off on West River Boulevard at 4:30 a.m. on Wednesday with my rifle. Through the phone app, I watched him sleep until his alarm went off at 6:00. He got a cup of coffee and returned to his bedroom for a shower.

I couldn't see inside the bathroom, but he took a long shower. With sensitive skin, I also shave in the shower, so that wasn't strange to me. I heard a distant siren—then another—and more. I turned around to look towards the Boulevard and three police cars screamed past. A fourth one pulled into the muddy access road directly behind my car. He exited his car with his pistol drawn and approached me like a prowler.

"Put the weapon down."

I did as he said. He adjusted his grip on his pistol but didn't give further instructions until he was three feet away from me. My hands were out to my sides. I shifted my weight slightly but didn't move more than was necessary. He looked towards the River House, then back at me. He looked at the raging Placid River, then to me again. Sirens wailed from all over Mount Placid. The officer's gaze relaxed. He slowly lowered his pistol just enough for me to see his badge. Todd Merritt, Chief of Police.

He returned his pistol to its holster, tipped his hat slightly and nodded once. I nodded back and he returned to his squad car.

"Chief," I called out just before he ducked away into the car.

He stood with one hand on the roof of his car and the other on the top of the door.

"There's another body, isn't there?"

He nodded.

I looked towards the River House and took a breath to say, "It's not him," but the words didn't come out. When I turned back to Chief Merritt, he closed his door and backed out.

I unlocked my phone and sent a message to Sam.

6:23 A.M.

Assignment Terminated. Wrong guy.

Chapter 4

Midway

Three Months Later: July 16 (Current day)

My name is John Wolfe. Fourteen years ago, my daughter was kidnapped, raped, beaten and murdered. I don't like people. None of them. I've lived by myself since my wife left me when I reached an unhealthy level of depression after Katie was killed. I wasn't there for her when she needed me most. That kind of shit changes a person. I had to say goodbye to her in the Coroner's office after making a positive identification, then I said goodbye to my old self. That version of me had to go away, and I haven't seen him since.

I'm in, what you might call, a special line of work. I find horrible people, watch them, then kill them. The case I closed this morning was at the Mountainview Motel. A couple of fat bastards thought it would be a good idea to kidnap and torture a newlywed couple passing through, in their room. Room

23. This isn't a game, so I don't want to make light of it, but—I won. I always do. I left the motel a little while ago. When I have an assignment, something is terminated every time. Sometimes, it's the assignment; other times, it's the subject—both subjects in the case I just left.

After each case, and before I go to my home, I spend time at a midway. This morning, I rented a secluded cabin in the woods. I don't know how long I'll be here. I need to be alone. A guy in this line of work rarely knows if they're going crazy unless they have uninterrupted time. Time to think. Time to reflect. Time to transition. I can't just go back to my normal life. The mind has to make a shift. In the past few days, I watched those voyeuristic, sick-ass rednecks plan their attack—then carry it out. The one in charge tortured a young girl. He peeled the skin off her legs and hung it to dry on a display on his wall. Things like that will mess someone up for a really long time. I don't know what will become of that young couple. I'm no shrink, so I can't even wager a guess. That was two hours ago, right after I shot and killed the two bastards that kidnapped them.

Am I biased because of what happened to my daughter? You're goddamn right, I am. In the cases of a sexual predator, I believe my personal bias makes me good at it. I wasn't there for my daughter. Some days, I couldn't give a shit about someone else's daughter, but most days, it helps me heal. I hope Katie looks down on her old man and approves, regardless of my failure as her father the first day of her Senior year; the last time I saw her alive.

This place I'm staying in is nice. One of the best midways I've stayed in. The sun is still low in the sky and I'm surrounded by woods. When I finished breakfast a little while ago, I arrived here and unplugged all the electronics.

36

The radio and TV will do more to make a person go crazy than it will to heal a dude's mind. It's just me, with this journal and the little voice in my head. He's been quiet lately. He usually isn't. I'll stay here until I know I'm safe. Not safety from bad guys or backlash from my actions this morning. I don't give a shit about that. The only person I need to be saved from is myself.

I write in here as a record of sorts. It's therapeutic. It helps sanitize the jumbled tank of mental sewage. I start with a clean sheet of paper and a fucked-up mind. When I'm done, it's the mind that's clean and the paper that absorbs the excretion.

After an assignment, I write about specific things. How did I feel before the assignment? How do I feel now? How do I think I'm going to feel in a week? A month? A year?

Thirty minutes ago, when I was eating breakfast, I learned something; something that bothers me terribly, but put me at an indescribable peace. Peace. Weird. I wouldn't have thought I would have described it that way. More on that later.

How did I feel before this assignment? Hmm, let's see here—numb. Kind of like the day before it started and the days before that. After a person has spent some time doing a thing; regardless of what that thing is, it becomes the new normal. Every new job presents an excitement. It doesn't matter if you're asking a customer if they want fries with their order or someone sent you on a mission to kill a person to save others. The person in the fast-food industry had some level of excitement to get a paycheck, learn something new or meet new people. Maybe they went into their first day knowing it was a career move. Although they're upselling fries on day one, they might have a dream to be a franchise owner. A week or two into the new job, they've learned the process, and that excitement fades. They start their shift and clock out before they realize hours have gone by. If someone asked how their day was, they wouldn't feel the same enthusiasm they once did, no matter how minor.

Killing a guy is clearly more impactful that up sizing a combo meal. That first one stays with you forever. My brain has forged a version of the guy's happy family of a wife, kids, uncles, aunts and cousins. My dreams show me fantastic versions of their future; a future I took away from them. Other nights, I conjure a string of murders that would have continued, had I not done my job. The events of my days develop into nightmares about terrible acts that would have continued if I hadn't stopped that man.

There is always adrenaline involved that comes from the circumstances and events that lead to terminating a subject, but the job itself? It's just a job that has become my new normal, and I've become numb to much of it.

How do I think I'll feel in a week, or month or year? —I don't know. Since these words are all together now, there's no way for you to know I spent twenty minutes in thought before I wrote that simple statement of *I don't know*. It's hard to predict emotions from one minute to another sometimes. I guess I don't think I'm going to go crazy. After reflecting, I don't have any worries that predict a future of insanity. I do my job and I do it the best I can.

How do I feel right now? That's a bit more difficult to answer. I feel like I was gutted a long time ago; like all my insides were on the outside, and the healing process consisted of being wrapped in bandages, like an Egyptian mummy. The bandages were constricting, but the bandages held everything right where they were supposed to until I was all better. I wanted to be all better. I wanted to heal. I wanted to have the bandages removed. I got my wish. The bandages were ripped off, but I'm not healed. Everything that's supposed to be on the inside is on the outside all over again, and I can't stop the bleeding. I feel like my best course of action is to pull my insides the rest of the way out and taste their sweet bitterness. A new hunger washed over me that I've never felt before, and it's difficult to explain.

I told you I'd come back to my realization at breakfast; the thing that I learned that brought a strange peace. I just learned who murdered my daughter. I spoke to him on the phone at the restaurant. When I hung up, I saved his number in my phone. The detective that was assigned to my daughter's case came to our house, removed his cover and told us they found Katie, but we had to identify the body. He comforted us. He arrived at the Coroner's office before we did that day and guided us through the unthinkable process. I fought against the idea and offered alternatives, like matching dental records, but there weren't any. There were no fucking teeth in my daughter's mouth to compare. We—Penny and I—my ex-wife, made the positive identification of the fresh corpse that laid on the table before they cleaned her up. She was covered in dirt. Her eyes were sealed shut. There were leaves knotted into her hair and dried blood from her mouth to her feet. When we left the Coroner's office, the detective screamed at the elected official, then joined us in the hallway across from the shiny elevator to comfort Penny, who was hysterical. He crouched in front of her, placed his hand on her knee, then took responsibility for the Coroner's actions. He went far beyond his normal duty to ensure we were taken care of; comforted. On Halloween night that year, he beckoned me to the woods where they found Katie's body and told me he was certain it was someone who she knew and trusted. It was someone who she was willing to follow into the woods. He introduced me to The Agency that night. That's what we call the organization I'm part of now. Penny had already left me, and I was alone. Any parent in our situation would have been lucky to have a man like that on the case. But like with any man, he had a flaw. Two days before we met him, he kidnapped, raped, beat and murdered my daughter. I called him from the restaurant this morning so that he knows I know it was him. His message to me? "Good luck."

Let's get back to the question. How do I feel right now? Enraged, naïve and vengeful come to mind pretty quickly. But, as I said, there's a strange peace that has accompanied the other emotions. Conflicted comes next. Do I take a leave of absence so I can return to Indianapolis to avenge Katie? Should I stay here longer? Do I find a shrink to help sort this shit out? Do I call by boss, Sam, to tell him what I've learned and him to put me on the case?

Sam. Shit. He sent me a message a couple days ago.

I scrolled through my phone.

> *I'll give you until Saturday to complete*
> *this assignment. I got another lead on*
> *the River House. If you don't have*
> *anything on the motel murders by*
> *then, I'll send you the details.*

In my fourteen years, I have never turned down an assignment, nor have I even pushed back. I wasn't ready for another one, unless it was Katie's case. I decided not to provide details.

Sam, something came up. I need to
return to Indy to take care of a few
things. I'll let you know when I'm
available for the River House again.

Sorry, John. It will have to wait. Two
more victims were recovered by the
amphitheater. You have my word that
when you finish this assignment, you
can handle your personal business.
Take as long as you need at the
midway.

Conflicted became more prominent. Could I carry out my mission with this weight on my shoulders? I feel like Brad Pitt's character in *Seven*. I don't let anyone get close to me, and I don't allow myself to get close to others. It's better this way. I won't have surprise boxes to find in an open field.

Sam's message was simple. His instructions were to be followed without deviation. I had to accept my new reality, get over it or suppress the emotions—for now.

I walked to the balcony of my cabin. It was on the second floor of a log home with modern amenities, lighting and electronics. I looked out at the valley in front of me. There was a thick white mist low in the valley and a cloudless sky above. Rolling hills surrounded me. With my head back, I took a deep breath and closed my eyes. Instantly, I imagined standing in front of Detective Fuller on that Halloween night fourteen years ago. I opened my eyes.

Sometimes, it's important to recognize that our current reality is far better than our imagination.

I paced on the wooden deck with my mind flickering between the pleasant scene in front of me and flashbacks of Detective Fuller, Penny and most of all, Katie. I sat in a rocking chair just outside the back door.

She was in her room upstairs. She was sixteen. "Don't EVER call me again, you bastard!"

I ran up the stairs and knocked softly on her door.

"What!" she blurted.

"It's your Dad?"

"Oh, it's you. You can come in."

I entered her room softly. She sat on her bed with her back against the wall. She crossed her arms, and her long, brunette hair hid her pretty face. Her shoulders shook, and she sobbed. I sat on her bed sideways and placed my hand on her shin. "Wanna talk about it?" I asked.

"Not right now."

I looked at random things around her room. Not to determine what the hell was going on, but more to waste a few moments with the nearly impossible hope she might tell me more.

"You okay?"

She didn't answer me. She sobbed harder. I stood briefly to get a box of tissues off her desk and handed them to her. She set them on her lap, jerked one out of the box and tucked it under her hair cave.

I patted her leg and said, "When you're ready to talk about it—if that time comes, you know where to find me." I stood and took one step towards the door before she stopped me.

"Dad, don't leave. Stay here for a minute, please?"

When I turned around, her makeup looked like she was a model in a dark, gothic photo shoot. When we made eye contact, she retreated into the hair cave. I pulled her desk chair out and placed it next to the bed facing her then sat down. "What happened?"

I stayed quiet. Although it was probably a minute, it felt like thirty before she spoke up, "Jimmy's an asshole."

"Jimmy—help me out here. Who's Jimmy?"

"Jimmy Curtis."

"He's your boyfriend?"

"Well, not anymore."

"What happened Katie?"

"He cheated on me with that slut, Charlotte."

"I thought you and Charlotte were friends."

"Well, not anymore, Dad." She stayed quiet for a moment then shook her hair from her face, wiped tears and makeup away with a fresh tissue and asked, "Why can't I find a guy like you? Isn't that every daughter's dream—to find a man just like their Daddy? You understand me. You understand girls. You understand Mom, you know?"

I didn't have a clue what the hell she was talking about. I didn't have women figured out any more than I could travel through time.

43

There was no way I was going to admit that to her. Not at that moment, anyway.

"Honey, I don't think that's every daughter's dream."

"But a Dad is a girl's first protector, teacher, and best friend."

I nodded.

"It doesn't matter, Dad. Do you have any idea what I want to do to her when I see her tomorrow?"

I was intrigued.

"I'm going to grab her by the back of her long hair so hard, I'll lift her off the ground before I slam her back down. I hope all her hair rips out and she's left with a chunky bloody scalp. Then, while she's on the ground, I'm going to kick her over and over and over until she begs for me to stop. Then I'm going to kick her more. I'll put a string around her neck and choke her out, then kick her in the face until her eyes seal shut, her teeth fall out and there's blood flowing down her neck and onto her shirt."

I jerked awake when she described the exact scene where they found her body. I didn't know when the actual story of Jimmy Curtis cheating on her changed to my own day terror.

I stood from the rocking chair and went inside the cabin. As much as I wanted to move on, a man needs to know his limits. The last time I slept was in the woods the afternoon before, during my last assignment. I was a mile away from the Mountainview Motel. Even then, it was the only five hours of sleep I got in two days.

44

Usually, when I choose a Midway, I take it as an opportunity to do all the things needed to transition back to normal life. This time was different. I wasn't going back to my normal life. Sure, I was returning to my home, but the River House case made my pending trip far from normal.

I stretched and yawned, then went into the bathroom to take a proper shower. The hot water streamed out of the shower head and steam filled the shower. I stepped in slowly until I was fully under the showerhead, then stood there to enjoy the luxury since the only shower I had gotten the previous few days was from a black, plastic camp shower in the woods.

That was Friday. I spent the weekend writing in my journal, reflecting on the motel assignment and staring out at the rolling hills from the deck of my cabin. I slept a lot, which is normal when I'm at a midway. When I woke up Monday morning, I felt anxious; idle. I called the cabin company and told them I would check out that morning. When I gathered my few belongings, I looked out at the mountains again for no reason other than to take it all in one more time before I left for my next assignment at the River House. My anxiety was a signal that I spent enough time at the midway. I had a job to do—and another after that. The first was for my boss. The second? Well, that one's for me.

When I left, I pulled up to an intersection at the main road and stopped for the red light. An elderly woman was at the corner with a stack of paper and a stapler. She held the paper to the wooden post on the corner and stapled the paper to it. It read, "Missing: My son, Ronnie. Last seen Friday evening before going to work." It had a poor-quality black-and-white photograph of a large man. The same large man I watched torture the young couple a few nights before. As I've said before, there are over 600,000 missing persons reported in the United States every year. Should we really find all of them?

Chapter 5

Come on In

Last Thursday (Four days ago)

The rain had finally stopped in Mount Placid. The river crested just below flood stage. Chief Todd Merritt bounced around as he sped his car along the pitted Rivers Edge Lane. His tires splashed through the puddles until he slid a few feet on the rocks at the end of Rivers Edge. He opened the door before the car came to a complete stop and hurried to the door. He rang the doorbell, then knocked loudly fifteen times. When no one answered after twenty seconds, he knocked again, then backed up to look around the house to see if there was any movement through the second-story windows.

"DOCTOR COOPER!" He shouted, then rang the doorbell five more times. He put his hands on his hips, sighed and dropped his head. The door opened.

Brent stood just inside with a dark green robe. He yawned the sort of yawn that tears develop behind tightly closed eyelids. When he opened them, he squinted, then stood confounded.

"Officer," he started, then looked around his grounds. "What's the matter? What's going on?"

Todd felt his blood pressure rise. His cheek bones visibly moved when he clenched his teeth. He wanted to punch the doctor. Just before pulling his fist up, he asked, "Do you mind if I ask you a few questions?"

"I don't mind at all. How can I help?"

"May I come in?"

"I'm not really prepared for a visit, sir. I mean, my place is a bit of a mess."

Todd blurted, "I assume you're familiar with the bodies surfacing downstream at the amphitheater?"

"Yes, of course. Everyone is."

"We recovered two more a few hours ago."

Brent covered his mouth with wide eyes and shook his head slowly. "No. Oh, God, that's awful."

"Look, I'm going to be straight with you, Doc. I've questioned every resident of Rivers Edge and West River Boulevard. No one has seen a thing. Your house is the farthest to the North. I need to find out if—I need to *know* if you've seen anything since you've lived here; you know, coming downstream."

Dr. Cooper thought about it with his hand still over his mouth, and shook his head, "No, I haven't seen anything at all. I don't have any windows on the

West side of the house, though. I can see a little through the trees to the North, but not much."

Todd stared at him.

Brent cleared all expression from his face, then dropped his head. He sighed. "You didn't come here to ask if I saw anything floating by. You're trying to figure out if the bodies are coming from further North or they're coming from—" he looked at Todd in the eyes. "Here, aren't you?"

Chief answered before he could come up with an excuse. "You're goddamn right."

Brent's eyes widened and his eyebrows furled. He peered into Todd's eyes for several seconds, then muttered, "Well then—if that's the case," he lifted his head higher and stretched his neck from side to side. His lip curled when he said, "Why don't you just come on in," he said coldly without moving his eyes away from Todd's.

Todd slowly placed his right hand on his pistol grip and returned Dr. Cooper's cold stare. His eyelids twitched when he tightened them. "After you," he offered.

Todd reached for the mic of his two-way radio. "Spicer."

The speaker squelched briefly. "Yeah, Chief."

"I need you to come down to the River House."

There was a pause that seemed to last minutes.

"On my way," Spicer replied.

Dr. Cooper held the screen door open with his body, swung the front door in, then waved his hand to invite Chief Merritt inside. They never took their eyes off each other.

49

Todd stood fast. "Your house—your lead. Besides, I haven't had the pleasure of receiving a grand tour of your—" he focused on the area behind Dr. Cooper's head, then said, "home."

Brent stepped just inside the door, then to the side. Todd followed him in. The screen door inched closed and clicked when it latched.

Chief Merritt looked around the room behind Dr. Cooper. It was a game room. Across from the front door was a staircase leading to the second floor. To the left of the staircase was a door with a rectangular window on it. Chief peered through the window at the cars in the garage. "You a collector?"

"Collector?" Brent asked.

He spoke slowly, "Cars. Are you a collector?"

"No, I just really like the ones I have."

Merritt looked around at what he could see of the garage. The floor was epoxy and there were no signs of cobwebs or even dust anywhere, not even along the edge of the floor or ceiling. In the game room, there was a dartboard on one wall with a neatly placed yellow throwing line on the floor.

"Have any lights down here?"

Brent stepped towards Todd and pointed at the wall behind him with a nod. Todd stepped to the side and Brent flipped on all three light switches. The first turned on the rope lighting around the bar on the end of the room and a dim light above it. There were four bar stools in front of the glossy-topped wooden bar. The second switch was on a dimmer and turned on the neon signs in the basement. The third turned on the main ceiling lights in the room.

"Is it always that dark in the corner by the bar?"

Brent slid the small dimmer up, which made the light a little stronger, but did little to brighten the room. Just before the bar, there was a full-sized pool table and cues neatly mounted to the wall. The only other furniture down there was an octagon-shaped table for playing cards.

Todd turned to look out the screen door when he heard rocks popping from the tires of a vehicle approaching on Rivers Edge. He glanced at Dr. Cooper and said, "Excuse me," before he let himself out to meet Sergeant Spicer. Two steps away, he turned to look at the doctor. He wasn't standing near the switches anymore. He wasn't visible through the screen door at all. Todd approached Spicer when he got out of his squad car.

"What's going on, Chief?"

"Well, Mike—the fine doctor let me in to have a look around."

Lines formed between Spicer's eyebrows and he didn't mutter a sound. Chief clarified, "Let's just say, I asked him —and he obliged, okay?"

"Whatever you say, Chief."

Todd turned back towards the house. Mike followed. Dr. Cooper appeared at the door again, just as Chief Merritt looked up. Brent opened the door and allowed both the men to enter.

Mike glanced around quickly. "You have a nice place here, Dr. Cooper."

"Uh—it a—it's a basement, officer."

Todd glared at Brent, then turned to Spicer. "Check the garage," he said when he pointed to the door. "I'm going to look around in here."

Mike reached his left hand to the door and his right on his pistol. He opened the door slowly, then stepped through.

Brent asked, "Anything I can help you gentlemen with?"

Todd glared at him again when he stepped further into the game room but didn't respond. He walked towards the dark area by the bar. He rubbed his hand on the shiny dark bar top when he walked around to the serving side. The floor creaked. Todd opened the two cabinets under the commercial sink, then the small refrigerator. There was a jug of milk, some limes, lemons and a shelf full of Miller Genuine Draft bottles. He stepped on the creaky floorboard again when he came out from behind the bar.

"You have a girlfriend, Doc?" Todd asked.

"No, why?"

"A sharp-looking guy like you? Wealthy? You have a nice house on the river—I'm more curious, why not?"

"I guess I don't have much use for a one—"

Todd interrupted, "You have no use for women?"

Brent sighed and said, "It's not like that."

"Then a boyfriend, perhaps?"

"No. I date occasionally, but I'm married to my work. I'm too young to settle in with a long-term relationship. To be honest, I'm not sure I'll ever want one."

Todd took a step closer to Dr. Cooper. "Why is that, Doc?"

Brent stood strong and said, "Look, I'm a single guy. I enjoy being single. Call me selfish if you want. I guess I just won't know if someone wants me because I'm a wealthy doctor or if there's something deeper. Better to stay single. I don't go looking for love, Chief. If it finds me someday, maybe I'll change my mind, but today is not that day."

Spicer walked in from the garage and shook his head once towards Todd.

52

"Nothing?" Todd asked.

He shook his head again.

"Let's go upstairs then. You lead, Doc."

"No."

Chief Merritt turned just his head to Brent. "What?"

"I said no. Your tour is over. I've let you into my house and all you've done is disrespect me since you've been here. If you want to see more, you'll have to get a warrant."

Todd stood in place. Dr. Cooper reached the front door and held it open wider. Todd didn't move from his position.

"Now, officers."

Spicer said, "Chief—it's time. Come on. The man said we have to leave. If we get what we need, we'll come back. Now, let's get out of this man's way."

Todd recalled the last text he received when he called the number on the blank business card taped to the underside of his desk.

> *Stay the fuck out of my way. You'll be*
> *notified when it's time.*

Todd glared at Dr. Cooper as he walked towards the front door. He paused, facing him before he walked outside. Brent looked up at him and said, "Look, Chief—I'm sorry as hell about what's going on in our little town. Whoever is doing this is twisted, and I'm disgusted by it. I moved here because I like this little place. I wanted to practice in an area that I could get to know the patients, although most don't remember me, anyway. They only see me a short time before I make them count backwards and put them under. I've been following this story since I moved here. The number to the station is on my refrigerator upstairs. You have my word. If I see anything coming down the river, I'll call you."

Todd turned to walk out. Brent grabbed his arm. "Chief."

Todd snapped his head to glare at the doctor.

Dr. Cooper pleaded, "This has to stop. If I can help in any way, please let me know. You can use my property to observe if you need to. There's a three-story deck on the back of the house. If your interest is finding the killer and not accusing me without grounds, you're welcome here any time. I only ask that you call ahead if you want to take advantage of the offer."

Chief sighed and Dr. Cooper let go of his arm. Todd offered his hand to the doctor to shake it. "Thanks."

Brent watched the two officers walk to their cars. Just before he got in, Todd got his attention, "Dr. Cooper."

"Yeah?"

"I'm sorry. You're right. You have my word that I won't stop until I catch this bastard."

Brent nodded and Todd ducked into his car. Sergeant Spicer followed. When they pulled away, Todd called Spicer on his cell phone.

"Yeah Chief?"

"Well, damn," is all he said.

"I know, Chief. We'll get him. We've underestimated whoever is doing this. They've made it look like the doctor to keep us off their trail."

"Mike, I've been on the force for a long time. How could I have been so wrong? I was just certain it was him."

"I don't mean any disrespect, sir, but let me caution you. Don't be as sure that it's not him as you were that it was. He could still be involved. We can't afford to be certain of anything."

"I know. Thanks, Mike—hey off topic, when did Charlie Branson move out? There's a FOR SALE sign in his yard and the place looks deserted."

"Hell, he moved out right after the last flood. I think he emptied it and left the mess from the flood. He was probably sick of cleaning up the mess."

"Damn. The Branson's have lived here forever. I think that house was where his grandparents lived. Shit, maybe even his great grandparents."

"That's life as a river rat, Chief. They raise kids here and create a million memories. When those kids grow up, and their parents pass, they want to give their own kids the same memories."

"Yeah—I guess you're right about that. It's a pain in the ass for us, but The Fourth of July is always a good time on the river with the Yacht Club's fireworks."

"All those goddamn boats tied up together," Mike laughed. "I bet the river is yellow downstream that night."

Todd laughed. Mike said, "When we're done at the amphitheater, let's meet at the station. We'll look through that file again. I'll help you."

The entire police force was at the amphitheater when they arrived. The current in the river was fast. Mike and Todd ducked under the yellow perimeter tape and went inside the walls of the blue tarp.

"Dammit," Merritt said. "One's not enough anymore. This bastard has to take two at a time. One's too easy now. It's like an addiction." He looked around the scene, then called out, "Where are the victims?"

Baker replied, "They're over here, Chief."

He walked to the gurneys, then glanced around to make sure no one would see when he pulled the sheet away. He stood between the two and looked them over. "Anything new, Baker?"

"No. They're the same as the others. Lines on their necks, some obvious signs of a fight, a couple of bruises and glossy eyes."

He pulled the sheets down to their feet. The woman on the left gurney had long, curly blonde hair. The one on the right was a brunette with hair that barely covered the back of her neck. Baker joined him.

"We'll get them to the Coroner to see if they find anything new, but I couldn't see any differences."

"Damn, what is this now? Eleven?"

"Yeah."

Todd looked over each of the victims in detail. "Have you taken pictures?" Baker confirmed.

He looked at their pale white skin. From their feet to their head, he scanned every inch of them and noticed a few bruises on their legs, the line around their neck and their whited-out, glossy eyes. He stared into each of them. The blonde, then the brunette, and the blonde again. He tilted his head to the side and called out, "Baker?"

"Yeah, Chief," he heard from fifty feet away.

"Did you get close ups of their eyes?"

"I think so." He turned the camera on and scrolled through the photos he took. "Yeah, here they are." He turned the display of the camera towards Todd.

He put both of his hands on top of his head and called out, "MIKE!"

56

Sergeant Spicer ran to him, "Yeah?"

"We're too late."

Spicer looked at the victims, then at Todd twice with his eyebrows furled and said, "Uh—Chief?"

"Look," he said and pointed to their eyes. "Glossy and white."

Still confused, Mike asked, "Okay?"

"Each of the victims recovered from the river had iridescent eyes. How much color in them has varied some from one victim to the next. These two—almost completely white."

"Yes?" Spicer asked.

"They were already dead on the first day of rain. We're too late." He looked at the other officers and shouted, "MATTHEWS!"

"Over here, Chief."

"Get your diving gear and gather a team. Look here." He pointed to the wrinkled skin on the victims. "Their skin is soft. Not just a little. It's saturated."

"What's that supposed to mean?" he asked.

"They weren't just thrown into the river. They were held under the water for hours—maybe days before they were released to be carried with the current. Dammit, dammit, DAMMIT!"

He looked around the banks of the river and focused on expressions of the onlookers. Some were on their phones, and others stood crying.

"HURRY UP! Let's get this cleared out."

He drove away in his car but didn't go straight to the station. He took the long way. East on River Road, North to the cross street over the river, West to West River Boulevard, then South to a small pull-off on the left side of the road. He pulled off the road into a small, wooded area, then looked around to ensure he wasn't seen. When he knew it was clear, he retrieved the strange card from his wallet and dialed the number.

When it stopped ringing, he said, "Two more bodies were just recovered from the Placid River. Please send a new contract."

After a long silence, the digitized voice responded, "You were wrong last time, and it cost you a quarter of a million dollars. If you're wasting my time again, it will be your head I'll request. I hope you're sure this time."

There was another uncomfortable silence. The voice continued, "Same suspect?"

Chief Merritt thought about his exchange with Dr. Cooper only thirty minutes before as he stared across the river at the doctor's house. He replayed the departing conversation, then he thought about Mike Spicer's warning. *Don't be as sure that it's not him as you were that it was. He still could be involved. We can't afford to be certain of anything.*

He finally replied, "Yes."

Chapter 6

Tick-Tock

Monday, July 16 (Current Day)

It's strange, isn't it? The elderly woman is posting signs on street corners to help find a man she loved, her son. For a moment, Ronnie wasn't just another criminal. He was a son. Perhaps a brother. Maybe even a father. Here's a woman stapling 'Missing' posters to telephone poles, and I'd rather piss on his bones than look at him. We all have enemies. We all have loved ones. I guess if I think hard enough about it, I can conclude that everyone feels loved by some and hated by others. There are many characters inside each of us. We show one to some and a different one to others. Did Detective Fuller hate Katie? Is that why he killed her. Is he just another twisted fuck serial killer, or was Katie his only victim?

I have never killed a man that wasn't an assignment. I killed in Afghanistan wearing a uniform before I killed men for The Agency. There was a time between those that all I wanted was to live a peaceful life. Since Katie's murder, I've dreamt about different ways I would kill the man who did it. Some are far more heinous than others, but in my dreams, I could never identify a single perpetrator. I imagined him with unfamiliar faces at different times. Sometimes, he had clean, inconspicuous features. Other times, I looked into his eyes and knew he was fucking crazy. I've killed him fast with a bullet. I've killed him slowly with a rusty knife. Fuck, in one dream, I even tore him apart limb by limb, then sent pieces of him to murderers as a warning. One package for each finger, two for his eyeballs, one for what I left of his head and others with pieces of arms and legs. I partnered each with a diagram that showed the location from which I removed the body part.

All of that changed Friday morning. Now, her killer has a face. I know exactly who it is—and I've dreamt about him both nights since.

As I drove the interstate, I tried to focus on the details of the River House murders. I thought of Sam's message from Thursday. It was vague and only said he had another lead on the River House. I haven't received a follow-up message with details. I glanced between the highway and my satellite phone to see if there was a new secure podcast to download. It took me two miles of glancing between the road and my phone to get to the right app, but I got the confirmation I was looking for. There wasn't a new podcast. This was a unique assignment, though. It was the first one that I was returning to after previously terminating, because they had the wrong guy.

I couldn't get Fuller out of my mind. When I tried to imagine Dr. Brent Cooper, I saw his house, his Corvette, and his game room, but as much as I tried to imagine his face, I only saw Fuller as the resident. I spent the next few miles sending another message, one letter at a time.

> Sam, shouldn't someone else take
> the River House case since I live
> there, and I was there three months
> ago?

Twenty miles later, my phone vibrated.

No

I would not try again. In my former life, I was a manager of professional corporate trainers. The company I worked for gave enough time off, that after twenty years with them, I could have taken a three-day weekend every week and still have enough banked to take Penny and Katie for a vacation. As a hitman, I didn't have the luxury of calling in sick.

Ah, I could finish this assignment and request retirement. I thought about that for several miles with the cruise control set at 75. The Agency doesn't offer a retirement package. There's no pension plan, insurance, or even a 401(k). There's a price on every contract. Forty percent goes to The Agency and I keep the other sixty. Back in April, I worked the case at the River House for a few days and banked $150k. The worst part of that assignment was all the damn rain. On the third day, it was over before I could do my job. Sam works up the contract and I'm not included in the price negotiation but based on the case at the Mountainview last week, I expect I'll likely have a package sent to me this week with at least $600k. Since there was a second unexpected suspect, that figure could be $750,000.00. Trust me when I say that money is not an issue. I could have retired many years ago and still not be able to spend all of it in this lifetime. I can't buy some elaborate house or big money luxury items. As far as the government knows, my income has reached $85,000.00 a year. Some of that is tax protected under a retirement plan and qualified health insurance. My W-2 even shows a benefit of using the company vehicle for personal use. Ultimately, $85,000.00 a year isn't enough to buy big luxury items and I sure as hell don't want to bring attention to myself. I'm not greedy either. Every year, I anonymously distribute a million dollars to battered women's shelters across the country.

The question of retirement seems easy, doesn't it? It's not. When I'm given an assignment, I'm protected by the very agencies that request my services. I don't know how the local police come up with that kind of money, and I couldn't guess how they pretend to investigate the cases assigned to me. I don't particularly care, either. It's not my problem. When it all comes down to it, I entered this line of work to find my daughter's killer and bring her justice. Detective Fuller is out there. If I'm retired, I'll be no different from any other murderer out there. I won't have that protection. He admitted guilt. Why not just report him? I have no proof. I only have his admission over an untraceable phone with no record that the call ever happened.

Besides, just for entertainment, let's play out the trial of The State vs. Detective Fuller. He had more on me than I had on him. The trial would expose the Agency and Sam would disband it. We've saved countless lives, and I needed to protect The Agency as much as I wanted to protect my daughter.

It backed me into a dark corner of my own dark mind because of my own dark decisions in the last fourteen years. If you back a man into a corner, he'll do unthinkable things. I had no choice. I *had* to work the case at the River House. My drowning desire for vengeance was prominent, but I had to suppress it, and I didn't know how.

As I neared the exit for Mount Placid, my thoughts shifted to my home; specifically, things I might need from the grocery store. I waste a lot of money on groceries that expire before I use them. I'm that guy who dumps milk on the expiration date. Don't preach that it's a recommended "sell by" date. I've drunk enough milk to know it just tastes different on that date. Whoever determines the freshness date on a jug of milk has to be a brilliant farmer and mathematician. I bet they have that shit right down to the hour. I've drank milk after that date and even though it doesn't make me sick, trust me; it's just different.

I passed my driveway and continued into town for milk, eggs, and bread, which are the items that usually grow penicillin and curdle while I'm out killing folks. It was an uneventful shopping experience until I returned to my vehicle and a police officer pulled his car in the space next to mine. I recognized him instantly, which wasn't an issue. He looked around the parking lot, then approached me when I put the bag and the gallon of milk in my back seat.

He reached his hand to me and said, "I don't think we've met. I'm Todd Merritt. I'm the Chief of Police for Mount Placid."

I responded before I could think, "John Wolfe. It's good to meet you."

The second I blurted my name, I knew I fucked up.

He whispered, "Boy, am I glad to see you again."

"I don't know what you're talking about."

"Back in April, I saw you—in the woods off of West River Boulevard."

I furled my eyebrows and said, "No, I don't think so. I—"

He got closer and lowered his voice, "John, please—this has to stop. Work with me here. We can do this. We can put a stop to it."

He glanced behind me and stopped talking. A woman called out, "Hi, Chief."

"Hi Betty. How's Tucker?"

"He's okay. Just took the cone off his head yesterday. You getting any closer to finding out who's doing this?"

"Mrs. Thippet, you know I can't discuss that. I'm sorry. We're doing everything we can."

When she pulled out, he continued, "I know everyone in this town. I know a stranger when I see one."

"I don't know what you're talking about, Chief. I've lived here for years."

He leaned in even closer and lowered his voice to a whisper, "Look, I know I'm not supposed to interrupt your work. That's why I left you alone in the woods that day. I spoke to the suspect on Thurs—"

I interrupted him, "If you know what's good for you, Chief, you'll move on like we never met. I'm here to do a job and I'll do that job if I see what's needed to do it. Do yours. Stay the fuck away from me."

I inched between him and the car, then drove off. When I pulled onto the street, I put my head against the headrest, "What were you thinking, asshole?"

But I *wasn't* thinking. In fourteen years, I've never blurted a name other than Roger Floyd; the name I made up during my first assignment and since, have identification to prove it. I felt a rage building inside of me. I wouldn't be so scattered if I was as focused as I should have been. My heart beat faster. My breathing was deeper.

I put the groceries away when I got to my house, then stood in my kitchen and stared; not at anything inside my home, but beyond the refrigerator, the walls, the grounds, the tree line by the road and far beyond that. I stared into the darkness of my past, angry at myself for not protecting my daughter. Angry at Penny for leaving me. Angry at Fuller for the horror he brought into my life, but above all, I was angry at the fact that I *was* angry, and I couldn't control it. Nothing could hydrate my insatiable thirst for revenge. I had decided. Regardless if Sam assigned the case to me or not, I was undoubtedly going to kill Detective Fuller. My phone vibrated.

> Hi John. I'm sorry I didn't send the
> remaining details. Not that you need
> them. They recovered two more bodies
> from the river Thursday morning by
> the amphitheater. Same suspect. I'll
> monitor you closely. I don't know
> what's going on in your life, but you
> have to put it aside. Let's close this

case quickly so you can move past
whatever it is.

I couldn't agree more with closing the case quickly. I put my phone back in the clip on my belt and retrieved my gear from the trunk, which was only a single backpack and my AR-15. In the garage, I stripped down the rifle and cleaned every piece. As I cleaned the carbon from around the bolt, I recalled the bullet used in the motel case. I only had to use one. One perpetrator killed the other. Then, when Ronnie, the man on the *Missing* poster signs, burst through the door of Room 23, I took my shot from a hundred yards away.

When all the pieces were clean, I put the rifle back together, then rushed around the house to replenish my supplies. Peanut butter and cheese crackers, bottles of water, and the single round that was missing from the clip. I put all of it into the trunk of my car and pulled out the black plastic camp shower to fill it. Once everything was ready, I walked around my house to look in every room but didn't know why. My best guess was to remind myself that I still had a home. As infrequently as I use it, it's mine. I pay the mortgage every month from the bank account I deposit into bi-weekly from the cash hidden in fireproof cases hidden throughout. I stopped at the doorway to my bedroom. The bed was tightly made and had been since last Tuesday when I got the message from Sam about the motel case. I don't know how long I stared into the empty bedroom, but whatever I was thinking about came full circle and returned to the River House. I pushed myself off the wall, got into the car and drove to the small, wooded area off West River Boulevard.

The air was scorching, and the woods were thick with foliage; much more than there was back in April, but I still had an unobstructed view of Dr.

Cooper's house from across the river. Also, unlike the last time, most of the docks had boats tied to them, including Dr. Cooper's. Not surprising, his was nicer than the others. His boat looked fast, even tied to the dock. It was narrower than most of the others and longer. There were seats at the bow and the stern.

I looked behind me towards the boulevard until a car passed. I followed the sound until the sound faded. Thankfully, I couldn't see the vehicle at all. If I can't see them, they can't see me.

I used the scope mounted to my rifle to see. It was Monday afternoon and Dr. Cooper was nowhere to be found, which was expected. I surveyed his neighbors houses. The first one to the South on the far side of Rivers Edge was a one story that was on the ground. I couldn't understand how or why a man would live along the river and not raise his house on stilts. I don't make it a habit of getting to know the people in town. The more I know them, the more they know me. When I got the assignment three months ago, I did research and studied each house on Rivers Edge. Ted Johnson was the most negative man I've ever heard of. He spent all his time bitching about everything. He bitched when it was dry. He bitched when it rained. He bitched about his neighbors not taking care of their properties. He even bitched about his garden that he worked in every single day. I guess he needed a reason to bitch about weeds or rabbits.

The next house was on the near side of Rivers Edge and across the street from Mr. Johnson's. The yard was neat and his house was clean. After the flooding in April, his dark brown house with beige trim was pristine, which is more than can be said for the house next to it. The last flood was in April, and

Charlie Branson still had a water line that surrounded his home. I scanned Charlie's property. There was a sign on the back of his house, facing the river. I held the scope steady. It was a realtor's sign. *That explains why he didn't clean up after the flood*, I thought.

Trees along the bank of the river and other homes blocked my view of the rest of Rivers Edge. I set my rifle down and considered how I would approach the doctor's house this time. I wasn't certain of his schedule. When I studied him before, he worked at the hospital on Wednesdays. Sometimes late. The other days of the week, he ran when he woke up, drank a protein shake and worked from eight to five. It was too late that day to disable his security system and mount cameras. I stayed there until after he turned in for the night.

There were aspects of that assignment that made it easy. Mainly, my car was quiet and the road noise on the boulevard silenced me. The second, which gives purpose to the first, is that I could turn my car on and sit in the air conditioning when activity was idle.

Once I was in my car, I thought of the exchange I had with Chief Merritt earlier at the store. Why did he want to get involved? Was it a lack of trust in me, or did he trust me too much? Not that it mattered. I didn't care what the reason was; there was no way I was going to partner with him. If I remove all the bullshit, the reason I was on this assignment at all was that the MPPD wasn't successful at prosecuting Dr. Cooper. I've certainly never approached a situation I couldn't accomplish on my own. My job was simple. All I had to do was watch people, then kill them. I didn't need help with that. I guess every cop has their case that they just can't shake.

I watched all kinds of boats go down the river. From canoes, to small fishing boats, to big pontoon boats. It was almost 5:00 when my phone vibrated.

DETECTIVE FULLER

4:58 PM

Tick-tock. Tick-tock

Chapter 7

Dr. Cooper

4:58 PM (Mount Placid General Hospital)

Dr. Cooper entered the recovery room to check on his patient one more time before he would go home.

"How you feeling, Abby?"

The young woman was sitting up but crouched over with her face in her hands. She lifted her head and said, "Better. Still feel sleepy."

"That's why we ask that you have someone give you a ride."

"How did it go, Doc?"

"You did good. Your vitals were fine throughout the surgery. I've worked with Doctor Patton countless times. He's a good man. He's been in to see you, yes?"

"Yeah," she said through a yawn. "He just left."

"There's a prescription waiting for you at the pharmacy. Take the first one in two hours, then every four hours apart after that to stay ahead of the pain. That sucker was deep. If you don't stay ahead of the pain, you'll know it. That abscess was in an awful place. As much as possible, keep your thighs apart."

"My husband will love that," she said with a laugh.

Brent sat on a short stool with wheels and rolled in front of Abby. "Can you swing your legs off the bed for me?"

Abby sat straighter and turned.

"Slowly now," Brent said and reached his hand out to her. She took his hand and used her other to pivot on the bed. When she turned fully, he asked, "How do you feel? Any dizziness?"

"No."

"Can you look straight at the wall behind me? I'm going to tap on your leg at different places. Tell me if you feel it."

She did as he said. He tapped just above her knee.

"Yes," she said.

He tapped a few inches higher.

"Yes."

"Okay, now, push your gown between your legs and separate your knees."

He tapped the inside of her leg, halfway up her thigh.

"Yes."

He tapped on the lower edge of the bandage.

"Okay, that one felt funny. I know you tapped, but I couldn't really feel it."

"Perfect. Only a couple more. Can you lean back a little for me?"

He tapped the upper part of the bandage only an inch away from the crease in her leg.

"Same."

"Good. One more."

He tapped the top of her leg straight up from the bandage.

"Yes."

"Excellent. The nurse is getting a wheelchair for you. Doctor Patton told your husband to pull the car around. When she comes with the wheelchair, she'll remove the I.V." He stood and moved over to the computer to make notes. When he finished, he said, "Do you remember where your clothes are?"

"Yes, they're in a plastic bag in that cabinet beside you."

He reached for the bag and handed it to her. "When the nurse comes in, she'll help you if you need it, then we're just waiting for Doctor Patton to release you."

"Thanks Doctor Cooper."

"You're welcome. If you get dizzy or feel nauseous, you're probably moving around too much. Take it easy, okay?"

"I can do that. I'm going to make Rick put on movies for me."

Brent smiled, "That's a great idea." He reached his hand out to shake hers and said, "Call if you have any concerns," then walked out of the room. He passed Doctor Patton in the hall.

"Doctor Cooper. How is she?"

"She's good. All ready to go."

"Excellent. You doing anything fun tonight?"

Brent laughed. "Uh, yeah."

"Uh oh. Sounds like there's a story here."

"I'm meeting a girl for a date."

Dr. Patton smiled and said, "Really? Where did you meet her?"

Bent laughed again. "I haven't yet. We met online."

"You'll be single your whole life. I can't imagine you settling down with anyone. A sharp looking young guy like you? Not a chance."

"Just because I'm not ready to settle down doesn't mean I'm not always on the lookout for my next victim."

Dr. Patton laughed as he walked away, "Oh boy. Good luck."

"Thanks. Have a good night."

"You too, Brent."

Dr. Cooper double stepped when he walked out the automatic doors and into the afternoon heat. He got into his Yellow Z06 and went home.

John Wolfe

It was 5:43 when the doctor finally came into sight. Thank God I had something to focus on other than Detective Fuller's text message. What did he mean? He was playing a game with me and I didn't know the rules. I tried to figure it out since the time my phone vibrated and felt like a little fish in a big pond. Fuller's text was my huge, barbed hook. I thought back to the phone conversation with him Friday morning. When I asked him why he did it, he said, *"Because it's fun,"* then, *"Now all you have to do is find me."*

He *wanted* me to look for him. He wanted the upper hand and, based on my mental state—he had it. For a moment, I even wished Dr. Cooper would kill someone that very night. Then, I could terminate the bastard and move on to my own.

The bright yellow Corvette disappeared into the garage. I opened the app, touched wi-fi connections, and scrolled. Dr. Cooper's wasn't listed, but more displayed as the phone found them. Mrs. Fields was one of the first. I wondered if I was too far away. But it couldn't have been. Dr. Cooper's house was sixty yards straight across the river. Mrs. Fields was almost two hundred yards to my right. It finally popped up as an option; b_cooper. I selected it and waited for the message. CONNECTION UNDETECTED.

Three months prior, I didn't have enough time to familiarize myself with camera locations. I tried to follow him through the house with the cameras when I connected to his security system, but it was difficult. From the first floor, I saw the game room, then somehow switched to one of the exterior cameras. By the time I found the one in his garage, he parked his car, and was already inside. I went to the previous screen and accessed the cameras on the second floor. I could have had better luck with the control panel of a DC-10. I saw the back porch, then a hallway, then an empty bedroom. When I finally found him, he was standing at the counter in his kitchen, sorted through mail, and threw most of it in the stainless-steel trash can at the end of the counter. He glanced at his phone, put it away, then got a beer out of the refrigerator. When he opened it, I tried to learn the order of rooms within his security system. I shook my head when I realized they were in order from the West end of his house to the East. They were in perfect order. As I was learning, it was much like the rest of his life. Clean; almost sterile, and in perfect order.

I found the Master Bedroom, the back porch, the hallway, individual rooms, the living room, then back to the kitchen. The Master Bedroom was at the end of a hallway off the kitchen. The sick fucker even had a camera in his bathroom that pointed at the huge, tiled shower. It was big enough that it didn't need glass panels to keep the water away from the main part of the floor.

In the bedroom, he undressed and put his scrubs in the laundry basket in the corner of his room, closed the lid, then adjusted the basket so there was even space from the walls on each side. He bobbed his head as if he were dancing. It was only then that I realized his security system was video only. There was only one way I would hear what was happening inside the house. I had no choice other than to access the house secretly and mount my own cameras.

He continued dancing naked into the shower and turned on the water. Once he adjusted the water temperature, he took another drink from his beer, set it on the counter and stepped in. I continued to familiarize myself with the cameras in the rest of the house.

By the time I checked on him again, he was already in his bedroom, pulled bright white briefs up to his waist, then scanned his closet. He retrieved a white, button-down shirt, black slacks and a jacket, then pulled out a drawer inside his closet to choose a tie.

I muttered, "Where the hell is he going? He just got home." I looked away from my phone and scanned his property with my own eyes. Another pontoon boat sped South along the river from my left to right. When the wake reached the banks, the floating dock swayed. Another harsh realization hit me. If he left his house, it would be impossible for me to follow him unless I knew where he was going. As fast as he got showered and dressed, I didn't trust that I had enough time to get to the end of Rivers Edge to track him—but I had to try.

I left my backpack in the car, so it only took fifteen seconds to put my rifle in my trunk, navigate the car to turn it around, then screech my tires onto West River Boulevard. I talked to myself the whole time, "Come on, John. You can make it. Don't bring attention to yourself, but for God's sake, get there."

Rush hour traffic had settled, but the four-way stops were a bitch. I kept looking to my right, as if I could magically see through the buildings and trees to get a view of the doctor's house more than a mile away. I finally reached the red light at River Road and turned on my signal to turn right. There was only one car in front of me. I watched the cross-street signals that seemed to stay green forever. "Finally," I said when it turned Yellow, but the idiot in front of me wasn't paying attention when our light turned green. I gave him a two-second grace period before I blew my horn and screamed, "It doesn't get any fucking greener, Jackass." Just my luck. He turned right. "YOU COULD HAVE TURNED RIGHT ON RED AN HOUR AGO, YOU DICK!" I rode his bumper in hopes it would make him speed up. I swerved so my left tires were across the double Yellow line. There was one oncoming car. When it passed, I blew past the snail in front of me. Not unlike others, I had to look at the person who held me up. For about a nanosecond, I felt bad. It was a little old man who was looking through the steering wheel. I was certain he didn't even see me on his bumper, and I hoped he was old enough that he didn't hear my horn at all and did not know I cussed him out—twice.

With empty road in front of me, I approached the sharp turn at the River Road Apartments much faster than I should have. That was obvious from my squealing tires, but I still slowed down enough to stay on the road after the ninety-degree left turn. Once past, I floored the gas and was at the entrance of Rivers Edge in under a minute. There was access to duplex houses across from the entrance with a five-foot berm separating the parking areas and River Road. I parked next to the berm, facing the exit, opened my window and turned my car off. A full thirty seconds went by before I heard the tires of the little old man's car mosey past with a string of traffic behind him.

It took me sixteen minutes to drive from the woods. I shook my head, certain that I missed him. The full length of Rivers Edge was about a quarter of a mile. Still, four hundred yards is a stretched possibility to tap into Dr. Cooper's wi-fi.

Options appeared in order of signal strength. There was an abundance of residents closer than the house at the end of the road. I scrolled through the list and found him towards the bottom with a single bar representing the strength of the signal. I opened the app, but the signal wasn't strong enough to view the individual cameras of his security system. Not being the type to give up easily, I selected the camera for the garage and waited, in hopes it would load an image, eventually. A few minutes later, the image refreshed from top to bottom, as if it were a sloth painting a canvas with a tiny brush.

"Come on, come on, come on," I encouraged, which didn't help. The top of the Tacoma came into view just before it froze again. A minute later, the full image appeared at once. The Z06 wasn't there. If he just left, I'd hear the engine revving to get up the hill as he approached River Road. I wanted to peek over the berm to see, but it was too risky. After listening for the 650-

horsepower engine for a few minutes, I knew I had missed him. He was onto River Road before I ever got there.

The sun wouldn't set for at least three more hours. I didn't know where Dr. Cooper went. He could have gone to the store for fifteen minutes as much as he could have gone to a nice restaurant for the next three hours. I couldn't take the chance to emplace my own cameras. Nearly defeated, I slouched in my seat and looked around the duplexes I parked next to. They were very well kept. The landscaping was perfect, from the bright green grass to the perfectly placed mulch around the bushes. The berm in front of me had a FOR SALE BY OWNER sign. *For sale*, I thought to myself. Just like Charlie Branson's house. I started the car and crept across River Road and down the steep hill of Rivers Edge. If anyone asked questions, I had a perfect alibi. I was there to look at the house for sale. I drove slowly along the pitted road and eventually stopped when Charlie's old house was immediately to my left. It was a small place; probably a one-bedroom that was less than 800 square feet. Across the street was Ted's house. His garden was perfect with a two-foot-tall fence around it. Luckily, he was nowhere in sight. If he was, he'd certainly wander over and bitch about a stranger's car in front of Charlie's old house. I focused entirely on the house next to me. Overgrown bushes surrounded it, other than the ones that were neatly trimmed where the windows were. There were even tall bushes on each side of the front door. To my advantage, there wasn't a realtor's lock on the doorknob. Even with my experience, those realtor locks are nearly impossible to pick. Even though it would have been easy, that wasn't the time to try.

My mirrors were clear. No one was visible, so I wandered around the place. The back had a beautiful deck looking out towards the Placid River. There was just enough distance between Charlie's place and the neatly kept dark brown house next to it, that I could see Dr. Cooper's house from the windows. Curious about my location an hour before, I went to the back porch to look across the Placid. The woods were thick, and the foliage blended together in a way that people couldn't see me at the observation point across the Placid. I glanced around again at the front of the house, paying special attention to the door lock. Nothing fancy. No technology. No code to enter. It was a normal, every-day, easy-to-pick lock inside that doorknob. Confident with my new plan, I left and returned to the observation point across the river and watched Dr. Cooper's garage closely through the app.

He didn't return until 9:22. When he pulled the Z06 into the garage, his jacket was thrown onto the passenger seat and his tie was loose with his top button open. He whistled a tune that I couldn't hear, threw his keys in the air and caught them on the way back down. Just before he entered the house, he walked to the passenger side to retrieve his jacket and threw it over his shoulder with a mile-wide grin.

Chapter 8

Reservation

6:18 PM (Three Hours and Four Minutes Earlier)

Brent took one last look at himself in the full-length mirror on the back of his door before he left. He straightened his tie, his collar, then grabbed the edges of the jacket at the buttons and tugged them downwards twice. Something else caught his attention, and he took a deep breath and exhaled slowly. He leaned close to the upper right corner of the mirror, moved his head from side to side curiously, then reached for a lint-free cloth from the inside left pocket of his jacket. With the cloth still folded, he buffed a tiny smudge from the mirror, straightened the cloth, then began to put it back where he retrieved it, but stopped before he tucked it away. The laundry basket was in the same corner, next to the door. He lifted the lid slightly, tossed the cloth inside, went to his closet, opened the drawer below where he kept his ties and pulled out a new, clean yellow cloth to put in his jacket pocket.

He glanced at his smart watch, hurried to the garage, then had the painful task to decide which vehicle to drive. The Z06 seemed to be most appropriate for the night. When the bay door opened, he started the Corvette, leaned back with his eyes closed, smiled, then said, "Man, I love that sound."

When he got to the end of Rivers Edge, he turned left on River Road. The engine roared smoothly when he pressed the gas. He took the sharp right turn carefully, looked at the clock and sped up. A car approached that looked as if no one was driving it. As he got closer, he swerved to the right when another car crossed the double yellow line from directly behind the other. As he passed, he saw an old man driving the sedan and flipped off the driver behind him. He looked in his mirror and watched the second car pass the old man quickly.

He arrived at the restaurant at 6:33 p.m. When he parked the car, he glanced towards the front door, but couldn't see inside the tinted windows where the woman said she would meet him. He inspected himself in the rear-view mirror, bared his teeth, then put a small peppermint disc in his mouth from a little round case he kept in the storage compartment of the center console. He turned the car off, exited and glanced once more at his distorted reflection in the window before he walked across the parking lot confidently. An employee opened the door for him to enter as he approached. His heart raced when he stepped into the cool entryway. There were several other people waiting for tables with round pagers in their hands. One of them started flashing as he entered, and the gentleman stood and stepped towards the host's podium. His wife shook her head when he walked away from her. Dr. Cooper turned to look behind him and made eye contact with a beautiful woman with light, ashy-brown hair. She wore a black dress that was low cut in the front and had a slit up the side that was barely separated all the way to her hip. She held a small purse. Her make-up was simple, a touch of eye shadow, some light blush and mascara. She didn't even wear lipstick. With one look, Brent could see that she didn't even need the make-up. She was beautiful. She smiled and said, "Brent?"

He stepped towards her, reached his hand out with a smile and said, "You must be Rachel."

"Yeah," she said shyly.

"You don't look like your profile picture," he said. She looked away, and he recovered, "Oh, it's nothing to be embarrassed about. Wow, I think that came out wrong. I'm sorry. What I'm trying to say is that your profile picture doesn't do you justice. If you don't mind me being so bold, you're—I mean—" He sighed. "You look great."

"So, you're saying my profile picture doesn't look great." She said with a grin.

"Th—that's not wh—what I was saying," he stuttered.

She grinned and said, "It's good to finally meet you in person, Brent."

"Do you want something to drink while we wait, or would you prefer to just get a table? We can order a beverage there."

She pulled her dress to the side slightly, exposing her open-toed right shoe. "These are brand new heels. If you don't mind, maybe we can get that table."

Even with the dim light of the lobby, he could see that her big toe was red. "Sounds good."

"Oh," she exclaimed. "I didn't check in to get on the waiting list."

"Nothing to worry about," he said and offered her his arm. She placed her hand on the forearm of his jacket and he led them to the podium.

"Cooper, party of two," he said.

The gentleman scanned the reservation list under the tiny desk light and began, "It's about a 35-minute wait if that's okay." Then he found the reservation. "Oh. I'm sorry. Right this way, Mr. Cooper."

He led them past several tables with guests at each until he reached a smaller room in the back. It was twenty feet long and ten feet wide, but there were only three tables in the room. Each table had a metal stand with a business card-sized white parchment in each. All of them had the name COOPER.

He turned to Rachel and asked, "Do you prefer the middle or an end?"

She glanced around the room and pointed to a dimly lit table for four on the far end of the room with only two place settings and a single taper candle in the middle. When he stepped in front of her, she looked around again and noticed that all the tables had two place settings and a single candle.

He pulled her chair out and stood behind his until she settled, then took his place across from her.

The host asked, "Can I start you with something from the bar?"

Dr. Cooper deferred to Rachel, who said, "Yes. I'll have a Gin & Tonic please."

"And for you, sir?"

"Pomegranate Martini, please with Belvedere."

"Certainly. They'll be out in about five minutes."

There was a pitcher of ice water on the table, which Brent poured for Rachel, then for himself. She pulled her phone from her purse and quickly sent a message.

"Was that a 'come save me' text or an 'I'm okay' text?"

Her face turned red as she put the phone away and she replied, "Uh, it was the 'I'm okay' text."

They both smiled and sipped their water. Rachel looked around the room again and said, "You must be a very successful salesman."

"What?"

"Your profile says that you're a salesman."

"Oh, that."

"What do you mean, 'Oh, that'?"

"I'm not really a salesman."

Rachel smiled with wide eyes and cast an exaggerated nod "Oh, I see. Do you start every blind date with a lie?" she said, still grinning.

"I guess so," he laughed.

"What do you do then, if you're not in sales?"

After a hesitation, he said, "I'm a doctor. Moved here a few years ago from Portland."

"I suppose, I can understand why you don't put that on your dating profile."

"What do you do?" he asked.

She took a breath to answer, but he interrupted, "I'm not talking about your job. I don't really care what your profession is. Once people find out I'm a doctor, they think I'm going to position them on some career status ranking board or something. You might be a scientist for NASA or a pizza delivery girl. I don't care. What I'm asking is, what do you do for fun?"

"Damn. You're just skipping the formalities and going straight for the personal."

"Aren't we just wasting our time if we don't?"

"Yeah, I guess. Before I answer that, you'll have to excuse me. I need the ladies' room. I'm going to leave my purse and phone here, so you know I'm not trying to escape." She squinted with a smirk. "Can I trust you?"

Brent laughed, "You tell me. Can I be trusted?"

She smiled and pushed her chair away from the table. Brent stood. When she stood straight, Brent heard something pop loudly, but Rachel turned away before either of them brought attention to it.

A waiter brought their beverages just before Rachel returned to the table. "Please try them and let me know what you think."

Each of them sipped from the small glass. Rachel spoke first, "Wow, that's fantastic."

Brent nodded when he placed his glass back on the table and said, "It's perfect, thank you."

The waiter smiled and introduced himself, "My name is Justin, and I'll be taking care of you tonight. If you can't rate me a ten this evening, please tell me what I can do."

"Will do, Justin."

Justin glanced at his small notebook and said, "Great then. I'll be back in ten minutes."

"What do I do," Rachel began. "Professionally, I work for a payroll company. I'm responsible for collecting my client's payroll data so we can file and pay accurate taxes and forms every quarter."

"Sound interesting," he said.

Rachel laughed and said, "Hardly."

She sipped her beverage and continued, "I guess my passion is softball. I love to play. I've been playing since I was a little girl."

"I don't know anything about softball," Brent admitted.

Rachel grinned, "Well, it's kind of like baseball, but with a bigger, softer ball."

"Oh, you have a touch of wise ass in you, too. I like that."

"I love playing, but I'm going to be out of it for a little while."

"Why?"

"Torn meniscus. I got it rounding third base last season."

"Was that the loud popping sound I heard when you stood up?"

"Yes, I'm so sorry. It's so embarrassing, but it's been so long, I don't even notice it anymore."

"Does it hurt?"

"Not bad. Sometimes it gets achy, but no actual pain. My doctor back home said I needed to schedule a surgery once I settle in here."

"Back home?"

"Iowa. I moved here a few months ago, but this is my first time out for something other than shopping. I do most of that online too."

"Mount Placid is beautiful, from what I've seen of it so far. You should get out more."

"I've heard they have concerts at the Amphitheater just North of downtown, in the park, by the river."

"Yes, they do. I haven't been to any yet, but I'd like to sometime."

"We can go together—" Rachel said excitedly before she retracted, "Sorry, I guess we better get through tonight before we schedule a second date."

Brent sipped his martini and said, "I'd love to."

Justin brought two more beverages. Rachel drank the rest of her first one quickly, then said, "Perfect timing," then sipped the new one.

Brent recognized her nervousness, so he asked, "You've been here a couple months, and this is your first time out?"

"Yeah, pretty sad, huh?"

"I don't think so."

"I work from home for a large corporation, but they relaxed some of their policies recently, including allowing people to work from home. It's not for everybody. Some of my teammates thought it would be exciting, but they end up with cabin fever. Their house is their office and their home. I don't understand that a bit. I could stay home all the time. I'm addicted to online shopping and don't leave my house at all, really."

"Oh, come on," Brent stated. "You *have* to have friends around here, I'm sure of it."

"Well, don't be *too* sure, because you'd be wrong. I swear it, this is the first time I've been out of my house, other than a quick drive-through or a fast trip to the store to get something I can't order online."

Dr. Cooper tapped his glass.

87

"What about you? What kind of doctor are you, anyway? A family Doctor? Wait, let me guess. With my luck, you're a gynecologist. I happen to be in the market," she laughed.

"I'm an anesthesiologist and primarily oversee procedures for orthopedic surgeons. If I'm lucky, I may see you again when you get that knee fixed."

They each sipped their beverages in silence for a moment until Rachel blurted, "What do you want?"

Brent almost spit his martini across the table. When he composed himself, he asked, "What do you mean? What do I want from what?"

"All this. The dating profile, going on blind dates, which, by the way, are usually awful."

"Yes, they are. They're impossible." He paused and answered Rachel's question. "I guess I want the same thing as you do, if I may assume."

She leaned back and said, "Have at it."

"I don't get out much, either. I don't really like to, I guess. This is a small town. In some ways, I love it here, but in other ways, I'd rather keep to myself. Like, in Portland, you can go to the same places all the time and never recognize anyone there. If that's the case, they can't recognize me, either."

"So, you hide from people."

"Not 'hide,' but I guess just don't like the small-town persona that everybody knows everybody's business. Let's use tonight as an example. If I socialized a lot, I'd get back home and all my neighbors would sit on their porches waiting for me to get home. What time I get home will determine how good of a date they think I had."

Rachel laughed.

"I'm serious. That's the small-town mentality. There's not enough to do to keep everyone busy, so they meddle in everyone else's bullshit. Excuse me, but it's the truth."

Rachel put her hand up, laughed and said, "Don't worry about it. It *is* bullshit." She crossed her right leg over her left. Her dress fell on each side of her leg at the edge of the table. Brent glanced, but figured he was fast enough that she didn't notice, then continued, "What about you? What was it like in Iowa? Do you keep in contact with your friends back home?"

"I did for a while, but you know how it is. Once you leave, you're the outsider. It hasn't been the same, but here's what I don't understand." She leaned her elbows on the table, sipped her Gin and said, "When I talk to my old friends, they tell me about what they all did together and how they wished I was with them." She circled the tip of her finger on the rim of her glass and stared at it. "Maybe they do it to make me feel better to let me know they miss me, but the truth is—" she looked up again. "It pisses me off. I don't want them to stop having fun and not go about their lives because I left, but the truth is, when they tell me how much fun they had, I just get mad."

"So, stop calling them."

"What?"

"If they make you feel worse about yourself, stop calling them. Don't put yourself through it."

"You know, Doctor Brent Cooper, you just might be right." She drank the rest of her gin and tonic as Justin came to take their orders.

While Rachel was ordering with the menu covering her face, Brent quickly reached for his cell phone and activated the video from his lap, then placed the phone face-down on the table. When Brent finished ordering, he pulled the napkin from his lap, touched it to his mouth and said, "Excuse me. I'll be right back," then placed the napkin on top of the phone.

He went to the Men's Room. When he finished, he washed his hands and returned to the table. There was a small loaf of bread with a knife in the middle of the table and fresh drink orders. He sat down, pulled the napkin from the table and placed it in his lap.

"Bread?" he asked.

"Yes, I'd love some. I'm starving and these drinks are really smooth." She sipped from the glass and said, "Maybe too smooth. A little food to soak up the alcohol wouldn't hurt one little bit."

Brent smiled as he retrieved his phone, pulled it behind the table, turned off the video and put it back in his belt clip.

"How many blind dates have you been on?" Rachel asked.

"Um—how many have you been on?"

"Oh, no. You've been on a lot, haven't you?"

"Why aren't you answering me?" he asked.

"Well, you haven't answered either, and I asked first."

"Okay, on the count of three, just blurt out your number."

She smiled and said, "Playful—I like it."

"One—two—three."

Rachel said "None" at the same time Brent said, "One."

Rachel was faster when she asked, "One including this one?"

"Yeah—including this one. I've only been on the dating app for a couple weeks. Wait a minute. Didn't you say blind dates were awful?"

"Yes, I did. Everything about this one was awful right up to the time you walked in and our eyes connected." She leaned back again and said, "Oh, listen to me. Liquid courage, I shut you down."

Brent smiled.

"You can't leave me hanging like that, Doctor Brent Cooper. Throw me a bone here. How's it going for you so far?"

"Can I be completely honest?"

"No, lie to me. Please. I love it when guys do that."

Brent shook his head and said, "This isn't a pity party. I'm not looking for sympathy or anything, but I can't tell you how many times women have taken advantage of me."

"Taken advantage of? I thought guys liked that."

Brent didn't smile that time. He continued, "Not like that."

"Have you been married before?" Rachel asked.

"Almost—twice. I tend to fall for someone too quickly then get my heart broken."

Rachel threw her napkin on the table playfully and said, "That's my cue. I'm out."

Brent laughed when she settled again and said, "Okay, not *that* quickly. After the second one, I decided that a serious relationship wasn't in my cards. I'm a young guy. Maybe I should just play for a while. Play the field, I guess, but even when I've tried, I just can't do it. I don't understand men who use women for sex or control them or abuse them—it's just not right."

"I bet your Mom taught you that."

"What? Hell no. I don't even know who my real Mom is."

91

"Stepmom?"

"Worthless. She screwed me over more than anyone. My own Mother, you know? I just don't understand how a woman can treat their son—even a stepson—the way she treated me." He sipped his drink and said, "Sorry. I didn't mean for this to turn into a counseling session. No, I didn't learn to respect women from any woman. I guess I just learned it on my own. I mean, I'm all for women's rights and gender equality and all that shit, but women deserve something a little more than equality. A higher level of respect, maybe. I don't know. The problem is that too many times, I've tried to show the higher level of respect and it backfires. Nice guys finish last, I guess."

"So, you're a nice guy?"

"I try to be, but I guess a person can't rate their own performance. They need feedback. Maybe I'm not a nice guy. Maybe I'm just another evil bastard. I don't know. Nobody's been around long enough to give feedback."

"Well, I won't pretend to know you, Doctor Brent Cooper, but my first impression is positive. I think you've been nice this evening. I feel like the only woman on Earth tonight."

Conversation faded when the server brought their entrees. When they finished their meals, they turned down an offer for dessert and Brent brought the date to a close. When they stood, he offered his arm again. Instead of placing her hand on his forearm, she wrapped her arm around his elbow and walked a little closer to him than she did before. They stopped in the humid summer air.

"I had fun. Thank you, Brent."

"I did, too," he said and kissed her cheek. "Rachel, I'd like to see you again sometime."

She smiled and said, "I'd like that, too."

"You said, you'd like to end up at the amphitheater sometime?" he asked.

"Yeah."

They looked into each other's eyes with an unmistakable and expecting stare. Brent broke the silence, "Goodnight, Rachel."

"Goodnight, Doctor Brent Cooper."

"You okay to drive?"

"Yeah, I'm fine. The dinner sobered me up."

"Okay, goodnight."

He watched her walk to her car, a dark green Toyota Corolla. When he reached the Corvette, he took his jacket off and laid it across the passenger seat, then loosened his tie and unbuttoned his top button. When he started the car, he watched her pull away, then pulled out behind her. At the first intersection, she turned right, and he turned left. She saw the silhouette of her hand wave as she turned.

He fumbled for his phone and opened the video he recorded at the restaurant. He saw the cover of his own menu, heard the end of her order, then heard his own order.

"Excuse me. I'll be right back."

The napkin covered the video, and he left just long enough for Rachel to make a quick phone call to a friend, if that was the kind of date it was. He heard the soft music that played in the restaurant. The ice in Rachel's glass rattled, and he heard her sigh occasionally, but she made no phone calls. As far as Brent could tell, she was truly here, in Mount Placid, alone. He put his phone away, pulled into his garage and whistled along with the song that replayed in his mind. The one from the restaurant that surrounded the air when he went to the bathroom. He tossed his keys into the air and caught them as they fell. Just before he entered the house, he retrieved the jacket from the passenger side and threw it over his shoulder with a mile-wide grin.

Chapter 9

Coward

Tuesday, 3:30 a.m. (John's Residence)

With all my gear in my back seat, I drove to the River Road Apartments, turned my headlights off at the entrance and drove slowly through the complex. When I neared the end of the parking lot, by the exit and the woods, I quickly backed my car into a parking spot. The observation point on West River Boulevard wasn't too far away from Dr. Cooper's house to move in when—*if* the time came. I scanned the windows of the apartments in front of me for lights. One was on in the second apartment from the end on the third floor. I watched for several minutes, but there was no movement behind the blinds to cast a shadow. I quickly secured my gear from the back seat, exited the vehicle and ducked behind my car, but still watched the third-floor window. The light was still on, but the stillness of the early morning remained.

I hadn't checked the weather forecast, which left questions in my mind. The environmental challenges I might face were unknown. How much time did I have? How long would I be on this assignment? Most importantly, when will he kill again? With the bank of the river behind me, I looked at the sky. It was peaceful. For a moment, I imagined what my life would be like if I had gotten up that early, just to get into a boat and go fishing. What if I lived in a house along the river? I'd sit on the deck with a hot cup of coffee and listen to chipmunks scurry and squirrels run through the scattered leaves under an enormous tree in my yard.

After I looked at the starry sky once more, I glanced to my left, right and into the river behind me once more. It was time. I ran to the edge of the property, into the woods, and ducked out of sight as quickly as possible below the crest of the hill. Once I reached level ground at the base, I stayed along the bank and walked towards the back of Ted's garden. When I reached the short garden fence, I stopped to scan the windows of each house on Rivers Edge until I knew it was clear. When I was certain I wouldn't be seen, I ran across Ted's yard straight towards the empty house that once belonged to Charlie Branson. I didn't see the doghouse until I was right next to it and heard a rapid, vicious bark. That Rottweiler burst from its tiny shelter like a bat from a cave at dusk. He reached the end of his chain and his body spun around only an inch before his massive canines sank into my flesh, and I kept running as fast as my legs would take me until I rounded the back of the Branson house. My heart pounded. My breaths were fast. I heard Ted's squeaky door open, and he yelled, "RAVEN, SHUT UP, GIRL!" The dog silenced and Ted muttered, "Goddamn rabbits" before the door squeaked, then slammed shut.

Next to the back door, I faced the river and leaned backwards until my backpack hit the wall, then tilted my head back and slowed my breathing. When it regulated, I observed my surroundings again. No one stirred. Few porch lights across the river reflected off the water and the night became still again.

It took less than a minute to pick the lock on the back of the house. The door hinge squeaked loudly and there was nothing I could do to silence it. My feet didn't make a sound when I stepped onto the hardened mud and silt that covered the floor from the last flood. After the obnoxious door hinge, it was a pleasant surprise.

The house was dank and musty since it was uninhabited for so long. I set my backpack down next to the door and retrieved the NVGs (night vision goggles) to look around. I was in the kitchen. There was a refrigerator and oven, but I was certain they didn't work. The darkened water line from the last flood spanned the walls and appliances a foot up from the baseboard. The kitchen floor was tile. There was an arched doorway into a living room and the front door to the house was on the wall opposite. When I stepped through the arched doorway, I looked to my right and saw a bedroom. The carpet was the same color as the river mud that blanketed the floor throughout. There was a window that faced South and one that faced West towards the river. Cheap blinds covered both. The blinds on the South wall were closed and rested flatly on the windowsill. The ones on the West-facing window were twisted open, the bottom only touched the sill on the right side and the left side missed the sill by two inches. There was a closet on the left wall when entering the room with mirrored sliding doors that were both pushed to the right side. I pushed

97

the button for the infrared light on my night vision, which acts as a flashlight when I look through the glasses. The closet had one wire clothes hanger hooked on the rod, but nothing else was inside.

I stepped through the doorway into the living room. There were two windows on the opposite wall that faced North; that faced Dr. Cooper's house. Neither had window coverings. The one on the left was useless, since the overgrown evergreen bush outside blocked the view completely. I put my back to the wall and peeked around the edge of the window. Dr. Cooper's house was in plain sight. I saw the entire front of his house. On the left, I even saw the garage doors and the carport with the hose on the wall.

My excitement faded quickly when I realized I had a full view of only two sides of his house. One with few windows that faced the river and the other with some windows on the second floor and a span of them on the third. Most of the action in his house was on the North wall I couldn't see, including his elaborate deck.

CONNECTION UNDETECTED

I viewed the camera in his bedroom first. The covers were scattered all over the bed and he laid on his stomach with his arms and legs spread out; naked as the day he was born.

It was 4:15 a.m. I looked around the rest of the house I was in. The front door opened directly into the living room. There was another interior door close to the bedroom door. I approached cautiously and listened with my ear pressed against it. After 30 seconds of silence, I turned the brass doorknob slowly. When I couldn't turn it anymore, I gently pulled inwards towards me. I stepped into the nearly empty one-car garage. A mouse scurried from the inside corner to the bay door and disappeared through the small crack between the garage door and the wall. There was a long extension cord hanging on a hook on the far wall.

Other than Dr. Cooper's, this one was the only house that had a garage. The others depended on carports or prayers that the full-grown trees wouldn't fall on their vehicles. I closed the door again and looked at the ceiling. It wasn't vaulted, which meant there was an attic. I searched the living room, then the kitchen, then the bedroom. When I opened the door to the garage again, I saw the pull string in the middle of the garage close to the interior wall. I reached to the string with an orange ball on the end and pulled lightly, but firmly. If there was a critter of some sort living in the attic, I certainly didn't want it to jump on me. The springs made a creaking sound with a rising pitch as they tightened. I unfolded the wooden steps until the bottom secured to the concrete floor, then climbed. Other than scattered rice-sized bits of mouse shit, the attic was empty. I closed the hatch and returned to the living room. It was 4:43.

If Dr. Cooper had an alarm set for work, it was likely on the half hour; maybe at 5:00. I sat on the floor between the windows with my knees pulled up and my forearms resting on each. It felt like an hour went by when I looked at my satellite phone for the time again. It was 4:48. *Tick-tock, tick-tock.* I pulled the cell phone from my backpack and viewed Fuller's message again.

"Tick-tock, yourself, you dick," I muttered. I put the phone away and checked the cameras on the satellite phone. I watched as Dr. Cooper's bedside alarm clock changed to 5:00. He didn't stir. I spent years in the military, which conditioned me to wake up at whatever time I needed to. I stared at the time for a moment, then locked the screen after I told myself to wake up at 5:30. If he still wasn't up, I'd rest again until 6:00. Before I settled, I stretched my leg through the strap of the AR-15.

Click, click.

With my head resting on my folded arms, I opened my eyes, but didn't move. Whoever pulled that hammer back and stood over me had the advantage in a situation I couldn't begin to assess. However, sometimes, when you know you're an asshole, a slight twist of crazy can get a guy out of situations like that one. I didn't move a muscle other than my mouth.

"You have no fucking clue who you're dealing with here. Put the gun down at my feet and I'll spare you an unmatched misery that you couldn't begin to imagine."

"Sorry John, you're wrong again."

I needed to turn up the level of crazy a little, so I slowly looked up from behind my folded arms and said, "If you were going to shoot me, you would have done it already, dumbass," then pulled my leg from the strap of the AR-15 and stood. "Well, fuck."

Chief Merritt kept the pistol pointed an inch from my forehead.

"Your name is John Wolfe. You were born in upstate New York; a small village called Springville. Your family moved to Indianapolis on Father's Day the year you turned thirteen. You were a failure in high school until your Senior year, when you squeaked by with a D GPA. You joined the Army soon after and were a lazy fuck. You had leadership potential, but never engaged. You gave up. You married Penny while on leave, just before your first deployment. When you got home, you got so shit-faced drunk, one of your buddies had to carry your drunk ass to the emergency room. You couldn't hack it and you gave up. When Katherine was born, she was your world, until somebody ripped your world away from you the first day of her senior year. Penny needed you, but when things got too difficult, you gave up—again. It's what you do. You run towards danger, you give everything you have, but when the heat is on, you give up."

"Don't you dare say another fucking word about Katie."

"John. Don't make this about her. This has nothing to do with her. It's you. You give up on everything that challenges you. You're in *my* goddamn town now. I called for help and they sent you. And John—I'm *not* going to let you give up this time. In the past, you've been a fucking coward, but your cowardice ends here. So, let's just skip past all the bullshit and get to the root of your problem, shall we?"

I did not know how Todd Merritt knew so much about me, but it made me very uncomfortable. When he said the root of the problem, I knew exactly what he was talking about, but I wasn't certain that he did.

"And what problem is that, Chief?"

"Fuller," he said. "He's fucking with you. He's gotten into your head. Is there anything else that could have caused you to fuck up like you did?"

I didn't respond.

"Oh, bullshit John. You left the back door unlocked, you fell asleep, and your cell phone fell out of your pocket. You're supposed to be completely unseen, but I keep finding you everywhere, at the grocery store, in the woods on West River Boulevard. I need you, John—but I need you to be at your peak. And let's face it; you need me, too. It makes no sense that I would see an agent like yourself, who's supposed to be invisible, in so many places. You're one of us. You live right here in Mount Placid. We have to nail this bastard. The stupid mistakes stop now, do you understand me? Now, tell me who this Fuller guy is."

"He's the detective that was assigned to us in Indianapolis—and he killed my daughter."

He lowered his weapon and cast a consoling expression.

John continued, "Yeah, I just found out last Friday."

His tone changed, and he nearly begged, "Please John. Let's work together on this. You told me the other day to stay the fuck away from you. I'll respect that, you have my word. I won't get in your way, but you have to engage in this case. It has consumed my life for years and has terrified Mount Placid residents. They've lost faith in the MPPD. What's your plan?"

"Look, you have no fucking idea what you're asking for. If we work together, I'm risking the agency's exposure and then I'm just another dumb-ass citizen and all the dirty work you hired me to do, falls back on your donut eating ass."

He pleaded, "And if no one knows we're working together?"

I knew he wasn't going to let it go. I had two options in front of me. Option one, I could continue to work alone, and he would keep getting in my way. That sucked. Option two, I could agree to give him information to keep him at bay. That sucked too but seemed to be the better option.

"I'll tell you what, Chief—I'll keep my plan to myself, but let you know what I have so far. You're clearly not going to leave me completely alone unless I throw you a biscuit occasionally. Every other day, I'll—"

"Every day," he interrupted.

I thought about it for a moment, then replied, "Okay—every day. At the end of every day, let's say midnight, I'll brief you on what I found that day."

"I'll call you."

"No. You are *never* to call me—*ever*. I insist on that. We meet here. That's my only offer."

"Okay. So, what do you have so far?"

"He left yesterday evening for three hours and came back whistling. I didn't have a chance to track him. I *just* started this case. Other than that, he sleeps naked. What the fuck do you want from me?"

After a brief stare down, I continued, "That's about all I know, for sure. I have access to his security system, so I can monitor every move in the house. His system doesn't have audio, so I need to get inside and emplace my own cameras while he's at work, which I expect he'll do within the hour."

"Okay, then. I'm going back to my car on the hill, and I'll talk to you at midnight tonight."

He walked towards the back door. Just before he reached it, I said, "Oh, hey Merritt."

"Yeah, John."

"I'm no fucking coward."

Todd snuck out the door and closed it quietly behind him. There was rage inside me. I hated Fuller. To some extent, I hated Chief Merritt. More than anything, I hated myself, because what I hated about Chief Merritt was that he was right.

I paced the length of the living room to clear all the bullshit from my mind. With my hands on my head, I looked up at the ceiling and paced from one wall to the other.

I love you, Daddy.

Her voice was as clear as it was the morning Penny took a picture of Katie and I by the car, just before she got in to go to school. When I stopped pacing, I reached into my pocket and pulled out the tattered photograph.

"I'll make this right, pumpkin butt, but for now, I have something else to do. I hope you'll forgive me for that."

I pulled the photo to my mouth and kissed it before I returned it to my pocket, where it's been for fourteen years, then drew my cell phone from my other pocket.

DETECTIVE FULLER

5:42 A.M.

> Time. It's a funny thing, isn't it?
> There's a time for laughter and a time
> for pain. There's a time for grieving
> and a time to move on. There's a
> time to live and a time to die. Your
> time is almost up. Tick-tock mother
> fucker.

DELIVERED

Chapter 10

Advisory

I went to the kitchen for my backpack and took inventory while I ate a package of cheese and peanut butter crackers.

Unless he was off that day, the doctor was within a couple hours of going to work. I had ten cameras in my backpack; not nearly enough to cover every area of every floor, but I didn't need that. I already had access to video of his entire house from his own security system. All I needed was audio, which I considered before I left my house that morning.

I reached under the extra clothing and towel, pulled the receiver out of my backpack and plugged it into the wall outlet next to me. Call me crazy if you want to, but I had to see if it would work. It didn't. I had a portable power supply in my backpack. If I used that, it would get me a few hours at most. I looked out the window again to see just how close the next house was. I

105

estimated there were thirty feet between the houses. There was a glow in the sky to the East, but the sun still wouldn't rise for another 45 minutes. With my NVGs, I inched out the squeaky back door with the extension cord from the garage, plugged it into an outlet on the neighbor's house near the back patio, and extended it through the window that was blocked by the tall evergreen. Inside the Branson house, I plugged the microphone receiver into the extension cord and checked each of the wireless mics. They all had a full charge. I guessed I had two days of charge on the microphone transmitters, depending on how much noise was in the house. After five minutes of silence, the microphones went into battery saving standby mode until a noise is loud enough to wake up any of them. As I connected my noise cancelling headphones, I wondered how a manufacturer could make a product that was wireless up to 250 feet, but not include an option for a wireless connection to monitor them live.

I picked up each of the transmitters with lavalier microphones and tapped the end of the black spongy cover. When I confirmed they all worked, I turned the power off each transmitter and the receiver.

At 6:00, the doctor's alarm woke him. He reached over to shut it off, then flopped face down into his pillow. Within a couple minutes, he stirred, looked at the time, then sat up. His face was dimly lit by the light of his phone. Unless he yawned or stretched, his expression didn't change. He used the fingers on both of his hands to type, but I couldn't see if he was responding to emails or text messages.

When he entered the shower, I accessed his perimeter cameras to identify potential methods or access that he could dump the bodies in the river without being seen. I studied all sides of his home to some extent before. The South side faced the length of Rivers Edge Lane. The front of his home was visible without obstructions of bushes or plants. The North side had the deck, and the West side faced the river. The East end of the house faced a large, flat grassy area, but I only knew that from glancing at it in the dark under my rain gear back in April and again a few hours before, when Raven came only inches from chewing my damn leg off. Jesus, she had big fucking teeth.

As big of a house as it was, he had four entrances: the front door, the garage, a double door on the second floor to a small balcony and deck access with French doors on the third floor. The security cameras had a view of each of them.

Dr. Cooper was out of the shower. He rushed to his closet and held an electric toothbrush in his mouth. With his left hand, he laid scrubs out on his bed, then went to his dresser to get the rest of his clothes for the day. With everything laid out on the bed, he returned to the bathroom. When he came back out, he didn't have his toothbrush anymore, then got dressed. He started walking out of his room but suddenly turned around and walked towards his nightstand to retrieve his identification and security badge and clipped it to his shirt before he walked out.

I quickly found the camera on the second floor and watched him get a fancy plastic cup with a flip spout and straw out of the refrigerator, then rush down the stairs. From the first-floor camera, I saw him enter the garage, secure the door, then got into his Tacoma. When he closed the door behind him, I put the phone down and peered through the window just as his garage door opened. The truck's engine had a fine-tuned rumble to it.

It seemed like an hour passed before I heard that engine roar along River Road when he reached the top of the hill at the end of Rivers Edge. My only remaining concern was the other residents along that broken strip of road. Rivers Edge had just enough of a bend in the right place that the only neighbors that could see Dr. Cooper's garage were the first two on the opposite side of the street. Beth Cummins lived in the second house. She was an attractive single woman who waited tables at the Placid Café that opened at 6:00. I peeked out the front window. Her Jeep Wrangler wasn't there. There was one other resident that could foil the mission. Ted, the grumpy mother fucker across the street that spent most of his time in his garden, in plain view from anywhere on Dr. Cooper's property, except the deck.

From the kitchen, I leaned on the counter with my business phone in my hands and accessed the settings of Dr. Cooper's security system. Each had an edit button next to it.

SYSTEM: ARMED (AWAY)

NOTIFICATIONS: ON (SMS, EMAIL)

DIRECT DIAL EMERGENCY: YES

HOST MONITORING: OFF

I touched the Edit button next to Notifications, turned off SMS Messages and Email, then saved the settings. Next, I turned off Direct Dial Emergency, saved the setting, then stood by the window that faced the River House. My phone vibrated, and a message appeared on the screen that read, PASSWORD REQUIRED.

There's an app for damn near everything, including breaking into a password. When I touched the button to find the password, it prompted me to activate the app that required a password. A second after I opened the security system, the scan started. All I had to do after that was wait. How long, I didn't know. The scan started with the lowest complexity, such as a single character, and progressed to more characters. If he had a one-character password, the app would have found it in less than a second. If it was up to eight characters, it could take 15 minutes to find it, depending on the complexity of the password itself. If he had a password of eight characters that was a combination of the alphabet, numbers and special characters with upper- and lower-case letters, it could take several days to find it—and I didn't have that much time.

I heard a loud squeak, so I peered through the small window on the front door. Ted came out of his trailer and walked down the portable steps. Raven dove out of her house and charged at Ted. Ted put his hands out and said, "Easy, easy, EASY." Raven put her paws on Ted's shoulders and licked his face violently. Ted's face damn near broke in half from his smile. "Okay, girl," he laughed. "Get off of me, you baboon."

He walked towards his garden with Raven on his heels and plucked tiny greens from the ground that were small enough I couldn't even see them from where I was.

"It's going to be hot today," he said when he rubbed the sides of the dog's head. "You're going inside when I leave."

I glanced at the phone. It was still scanning options to find the right password.

Twenty minutes later, Ted left in his 90's model S10. The roar from his truck was nothing like Dr. Cooper's Corvette. Ted's truck sounded like there was a hole in the muffler. It rattled and squeaked when he eased along the pitted road. My phone vibrated. PASSWORD ACCESSED showed on the screen, immediately followed by SETTINGS SAVED. I returned to the main menu of his security system to make one last change.

SYSTEM: OFF (NOT RECOMMENDED)

I secured my backpack, went out the back door, quickly scanned my surroundings, and casually walked around Dr. Cooper's house. There was a door on the back side of the garage that faced North. When the lock released, I turned the knob and slowly pushed the door inwards. Only when I confirmed there were no alarms and nothing beeped, I exhaled. I didn't even realize I was holding my breath. Just before I stepped through, I looked behind me. The tree line was quite thick. There weren't any access paths that I could see at a glance, but the water was close. I heard an engine on the other side of the trees and the distinct rhythmic splashing of the boat bouncing in another's wake. When the boat passed South, towards town, I quietly entered Dr. Cooper's garage.

I closed the door behind me quietly. I had been in many houses in my life, but none as secure as his. My heart beat fast. There was a loud noise. At the moment, it sounded like a dump truck's door slamming off the bed after dropping a load of earth. When I settled, I realized the air conditioner ticked a moment before it came on. *Get a grip, John,* I thought. Creeping through the garage, I heard a muffled engine of a boat speeding down the river. Then it was quiet again. The door to the house had a narrow window, through which I peered. With my hand grasping the doorknob in a tense fist, I slowly turned. My hand slid along the metal knob. I wiped my hands on my pants before I picked the lock and tried again. It turned easily. I pulled on the door, then stepped into Brent Cooper's house and secured the door behind me.

It was deafly quiet. No refrigerator ticking. No draft through the front door that was to my right. The silence was like standing in a small room with foam on every wall, floor and ceiling. I felt my chest pound with every beat of my heart. The only noise that broke the silence was the breathy air that exhaled from my nose. My eyes darted faster than I could comprehend what they saw. To my left were the stairs to the second level. My imagination emplaced the floor plan in the areas that I couldn't see on each side of the stairs. To the right was a large living room. Through a doorway, at the top of the steps, was his kitchen. To the left were the bedrooms, with his Master Bedroom at the end of the hallway. I knew all that from spying on him with his own security system. I took three steps forward across the base of the stairs into the game room. The entire room was dark, but the bar area directly across from me was the darkest. The only light source was through frosted glass high on his front door, the narrow window to the garage behind me and the light that beamed from the windows on the second level. None of which reached the back wall behind the bar.

I reached for the light switch next to the front door. There were three of them. Just before I flipped any of them on, I considered how modern his house was and the possibility that he may get a notification through text message of any changes to his house, from a heat setting, to a drastic change in temperature to any of his electronics being turned on. I quickly pulled the NVGs out of my backpack and peered through them as I walked towards the bar. When I first switched them on, my eyes squinted from the magnificent amount of light the night vision magnified. I set up the first of the tiny wireless microphones in the back of a shelf behind the bar. There was a white label on the back of the round disk with the number, "1." In the middle of the wall at the back of the shelf, there was another switch, but I didn't dare flip it to determine what it might control. I turned the night vision off and returned the device to my backpack. When I stood, I heard a creaking sound under my feet.

That's not possible, I thought. *He's on a slab.* I stood and rocked back and forth but couldn't recreate the sound.

My nerves settled, and I hurried up the stairs to the second floor. The kitchen was the central-most area of the entire house. It didn't take long to see that the cabinets were open on top and didn't reach the high ceiling. It was the perfect place for the second mic.

For a moment, just a brief moment, I paused and looked around his kitchen, into the living room and down the hall towards the Master Bedroom. There was no dirt. No dust visible at all and every piece of furniture, from a leather recliner to the tv on the wall was perfectly placed.

The wall opposite the top of the stairs had another set of stairs that led to the third floor. I recalled the floor plan of the top floor before I went up the stairs, two steps at a time. There was a landing and another short set of stairs to reach the open entertainment floor. Directly above the second-floor kitchen was a kitchenette with another full set of appliances and a door that opened to the uppermost part of the enormous deck with half walls with serving bars on them. There was a narrow space between the refrigerator and the wall that I placed the third and final wireless microphone. I looked around the floor and it was grander in person than it was as seen through his security cameras.

With the microphones in place, I calmly walked down the stairs to the second floor, turned to descend to the first floor, but paused before I took the first step on the last flight of stairs. It was a long hallway to the Master Bedroom. I trudged the length of it. Each of the bedroom doors were closed. Two on the left and two on the right before the double doors that opened to his bedroom. His bedroom doors were open. I took one step into his room but saw nothing strange. His dresser top was clear. There was a nightstand on each side of the bed that was raised one step up. Both nightstands were clear except for a lamp on each and an alarm clock on the one to the left, as I stood.

The air conditioner stopped blowing and the silence I heard in the entryway was hubbub compared to when the blower turned off. I knew nobody was in the house, but I crept back along the hallway to the top of the stairs to the lower floor. It wasn't until that moment I had another realization. I stepped on different parts of the floor; even bounced my weight a couple times. His floor didn't creak. Not even a little, and not one time. I shook my head and descended to the first floor, glanced around the game room once more and exited into the garage. Nearly at the small door into the garage, I stopped, then went back to the door into the house, opened it, reached around it and turned the lock.

I locked the door to the garage as I exited and looked at his elaborate deck. It was far more impressive standing next to it than from across the Placid River. Safely outside, I inspected every detail of the walls of the house under the deck. There were no openings, no crawl space or any other way to access the river secretly. The more I saw of Dr. Cooper's house, the less I believed he killed pretty girls and dumped them in the river, unless he walked them from his garage to the bank fifty yards or more from the door.

To do my job well, sometimes, I have to think like a bad guy. I returned to the door into the garage, turned around and walked towards the riverbank which I could only access at an angle. With each step, I observed my surroundings. Four steps away, I could see the windows of the Branson house. After six steps, I could see the front door and the pitted road beyond. After ten steps, I could even see Ted's front door. Let's assume no one pays any attention to the back of Brent Cooper's house from Rivers Edge Lane. At twelve steps, the houses across the Placid came into view just as another boat came racing down the river from the North in front of me.

When I reached the bank, I walked along it, and paid close attention to the steep bank that led to the river. There were no drains or any other means to access the water.

Confident I had done what I could until the good Doctor returned, I went back to Charlie's old place and tested the receiver of the wireless microphone system. With no sound generated from inside the house, all three mics powered off and became inactive. I felt a vibration on my hip from my personal phone but wasn't expecting a text or any sort other message. I thought I had turned off all notifications weeks ago. It wasn't a personal message at all.

Weather Advisory: Heavy rain will enter your area on Tuesday night and continue intermittently until late Thursday. Threats include heavy rain, flash floods, lightning, and high winds in excess of forty miles-per-hour. Expect the Placid River to rise ten to twelve feet.

Chapter 11

Behavioral Specialist

Tuesday, Mid-morning (Mount Placid Hospital)

Dr. Patton put the last stitch in the left side of his patient's right knee and Dr. Cooper pulled her out of anesthesia.

"Well done, everyone," Dr. Patton announced, as usual. "Brent, let me know when she's ready."

He removed his latex gloves and blue gown, washed his hands and left the operating room.

Dr. Cooper noticed the new assistant, Lizzy, looking at him and cast a smile toward her. Although she smiled too, her face became red and warm. She blushed, turned away and apologized. He brought no more attention to it, other than a wider grin when he reached for his phone to check the message he received during surgery.

RACHEL

Hi Brent... or should I call you Doctor Brent? LOL. Thank you again for dinner last night. I look forward to seeing you again when you're free. I sure as hell don't have anything else to do.

Hi Rachel. I enjoyed it too. I'd love to meet you again.

What are you doing tonight?

Sorry.

That was a bit bold.

Wow. I'm not like this, I promise.

WTH, I guess I'm saying that, with the rain the next few days, I'm going to be bored.

God, I sound pathetic.

Never mind.

You can lose my number. I wouldn't blame you.

Hi

> I'm sorry. I was in surgery. I'll check
> my schedule.

Just kill me now. I'm so embarrassed.

He turned back to the assistant, "What room is she going to, Lizzy?"

"Uh, let me check."

She pulled up a screen on the computer and said, "Recovery Room 7."

"Okay, thanks. I'll check on her in about twenty minutes."

"I'll let her know."

He opened the door with his back. It swung open, but he stopped before he stepped out. "Hey Liz?" he said with a smile.

"Yes?"

"You did good today. I look forward to working with you again."

Liz blushed again and said, "Thank you, Doctor Cooper."

Brent let the door swing closed behind him and walked along the bright corridor with his phone in his hand. He slowed his pace and peered farther down the hallway. Seeing no one, he turned to look the direction from which he came. He leaned on the wall, then lifted his right foot up and placed it flat next to his left knee. He glanced along the length of the hallway one more time before he sent the reply.

> I've been busy this morning. How
> much rain are we supposed to get?

I'm not sure. A couple days, I think.

He glanced up and down the hallway again, then continued the same direction he started going. When he approached the Men's room, he pushed the door open and entered quickly. All three stalls were open and there wasn't anyone else in there. He chose the second stall since the last was for people with wheelchairs, closed the door, then sat on the toilet so anyone who walked in wouldn't see the noticeable difference of shoes pointing any direction except out.

He sighed when he looked towards the ceiling, then opened the weather app on his phone. There was a dot that signified a weather advisory next to a bell icon at the top of the screen. He touched the bell and read the advisory.

Weather Advisory: Heavy rain will enter your area on Tuesday night and continue intermittently until late Thursday. Threats include heavy rain, flash floods, lightning, and high winds in excess of forty miles-per-hour. Expect the Placid River to rise ten to twelve feet.

He ran his fingers through his hair and read the advisory again. The door to the Men's room opened and someone entered the first stall. Brent reached behind him and pulled the metal handle. The toilet flushed loud and fast. Before he left the stall, he sent one message:

> Looks like my schedule is open. How about this evening?

He put his phone back on his hip, washed his hands and left the Men's room. His phone vibrated as he walked, and he checked the message.

Are you sure? I didn't mean to intrude.

I just get bored by myself, but I'm fine.

He grinned when he sent the reply.

Yes, I'm sure. I wouldn't have
suggested it if I wasn't. How about
my place?

That sounds great. What's your
address?

Why don't I pick you up.

He sent another message immediately.

IF that's okay with you, of course.

The smiling emoji response came immediately, followed by an offer of what she should bring. He shook his head and said nothing before he walked to Recovery Room 7. He reached his hand up to knock, but something startled him. Liz opened the door quickly and gasped.

"Oh, shit, you scared me," she said.

Dr. Cooper chuckled and said, "I'm not sure who scared who worse." He took a deep breath and stepped backwards when she closed the door.

"How is she?"

Lizzy's shoulders were still raised near her ears when she stepped forward and said, "She's okay. Looks great. She's starting to wake up so you can probably check on her any time."

Brent smiled and said, "That's what I was going to do."

Lizzy blushed, looked away and said, "Of course, you were. Sorry, Doctor Cooper."

"You're fine," he said, and she hurried away.

He knocked on the door to the recovery room and heard a voice slur a response from the other side that quite resembled a moan, "Come in."

"Can you tell me your name?" he asked.

"Ba—Bar—Barbara. Barb. Just Barb."

"Your last name, please?"

"Collins."

"And one more that I'm sure you'll get right on the first try. What's your birth date?"

"February 13, 1983."

He logged in to the computer to check Lizzy's notes and asked, "How are you feeling, Barb?"

When she didn't reply, he looked at her. It seemed to take all her will to get her eyes to open.

"Fucking drunk. That's how I feel," she slurred through laughter.

"Do you remember why you're here?"

"Yesh," she said, then laughed at herself. "I mean, Yessss. Sssss—ssss—Yesssir."

He grinned and asked her, "Why are you here?"

120

"I was bored over the weekend and figured I'd let Dr. Patton cut me up this morning. Thought it sounded kind of fun."

They both laughed and Brent asked, "Can you sit up?"

He turned his chair to her and said, "Slowly now. Your head will clear faster if you're sitting up."

He stood and held his hands to her sides when she swayed to an upright position with her own strength.

"You okay?" he asked.

Her legs dangled off the bed and she looked down at her legs. "What the fuck is this?"

"Something wrong, Mrs. Collins?"

"What—the fuck—is this?"

"I don't understand," Dr. Cooper said.

"Why is my right knee all wrapped up?"

Dr. Cooper's mouth gaped open as he scrambled to decide on an appropriate response. He finally said, "Mrs. Collins, you don't remember why you're here?"

She spoke clearly, "I remember. I came in for Doctor Patton to fix a torn meniscus on my LEFT knee."

Although he was certain, he turned to the computer for confirmation.

R Knee. Meniscus tear.

"Mrs. Collins, it's your right knee."

"Do you think I don't know which goddamn knee has been bothering me for six months?

"Ma'am, it says right here—"

"I don't care what it says right there," she interrupted. "You fixed the wrong fucking knee."

She pulled her long, dark hair back with both hands and stared at her knees, then instantly stood from the gurney. Her right knee buckled, and she dropped. Brent reached for her and caught her before she landed on the white tile floor.

"Get the fuck off me," she said, then pulled her arm back and slapped him on the left side of his face before he realized what she was doing. He turned slowly to look into her eyes, stone-faced, then let go. Her knee was too weak to support her, and she fell to the ground. He sat on the rolling stool again and leaned his elbows on his knees to look down at her.

She started crying, "Why did you make me fall. You pushed me down, you bastard."

He stared at her, silent for a moment, then pushed the call button on the wire attached to his scrubs.

"I need a lift team in Recovery Room 7 please."

He logged out of the computer and tried to open the door to leave. Mrs. Collins's head was in the path of the opening door. With the door against her head, he pulled harder, which made her body pivot with the door until it opened, and he walked out.

"Where are you going? Don't leave me here," she cried.

The door eased shut and hit her head again. She grimaced, and the door closed fully.

He moved his jaw back and forth and rubbed the side of his face while he walked through the hall. Two enormous men walked from the opposite direction. As they approached, one asked him, "Did you call for the lift team?"

"Yes."

"Everything okay?" he asked.

Brent considered telling him to mind the door when they open it, but only replied with, "Yes. I'll be there in twenty minutes. Stay with her."

"Damn, Doc; is she alone in there?"

"Yes."

"You know you can't do that."

He stopped walking, turned to face them and said, "Recovery Room 7. I said I'll be there in twenty minutes."

"You got it, Doc."

Brent turned back and continued to the Men's Room to wash his face and calm down. He captured the cold water from the faucet in his hands and splashed it on his face three times, then looked at his reflection in the mirror. He breathed deeply, but his heartbeat never elevated. An inch away from the bathroom mirror, he stared into his own eyes. Water dripped from his chin. He slowly shook his head, as if the man who stood in the Men's Room was replying to an unspoken demand from the man in the mirror.

He took two deep breaths, then pulled several thin, white towels from the dispenser. The first one only tore off the corners, which he threw to the floor, then reached for the rest from the dispenser. He leaned close to the mirror again and wiped the water from his face. When the towels were below his eyes, he opened them and darted his eyes back and forth into the eyes of the man in the reflection. His phone vibrated.

Weather Advisory Update: The severe weather system has increased in speed, but will meet a front from the South, stalling the system over your area. This advisory is in effect from Tuesday afternoon through late Thursday, which could raise the Placid River more than originally expected.

When he returned to the home screen, he noticed a small number 1 over the messages. He opened the app.

> Nice tactic, ignoring my message. I'll
> bring a couple bottles of wine. Do you
> prefer red or white?

Without replying, he left the Men's room walked to Recovery Room 7. Without knocking, he walked in and said, "Thank you, gentlemen. I'll take it from here."

The two men left, and the door closed slowly behind them. It seemed to be much louder than usual. He sat on the stool and logged into the computer.

She spoke sheepishly, "Doc, I am so sorry. There's no way I can sufficiently express my regret."

He kept his focus on the computer screen when he asked, "Do you remember why you're here?"

"Yessir. I had a torn meniscus on my right knee."

He glared at Mrs. Collins, "Are you sure?"

"Yessir. Everybody who talked to me when I came in asked me which knee, including you. I knew then, and I know now, it's my right knee. Somewhere under this bandage, there's even a red 'x' that Doctor Patton drew."

Brent completed his notes without speaking but glanced towards Mrs. Collins several times. When he finished, he asked coldly, "Do you have someone to give you a ride home?"

Barb glanced at him, but looked away, "Yessir, I do."

"I'll tell Doctor Patton that I'm done with you. He'll be in soon to release you. Liz will escort you in a wheelchair out of the building. Your ride will meet you there."

He reached for the door and pulled.

"Dr. Cooper?"

"What!" he replied without looking at her.

"I really am so sorry. Don't know what came over me. I barely remember what happened, but I know I wasn't nice."

He closed the door and sat back on the rolling stool. "Look, Mrs. Collins, it's common to have mood swings when coming out of anesthetic. Not incredibly common, but it's certainly not *uncommon*. Some say that how you act during that mood swing is like being under the influence of alcohol. It doesn't make you do anything you don't want to. It simply removes the filter, and we act based on our core instincts. Now, I can refer you to a behavioral specialist, if you think you might benefit from it."

She looked down and to her left, "No," she whispered. "That won't be necessary."

"You're sure? Deep-rooted conditions left untreated can cause a person to do unthinkable things. Your life can change—" he snapped his fingers and continued, "like that."

"I understand."

He stared at her.

She covered her gaping mouth with wide eyes and said, "You're not suggesting—the bodies near the amphitheater, are you?"

"If you say it won't be necessary, then it's unnecessary. Good day, Mrs. Collins."

He left the room. Doctor Patton greeted him with a smile and a loud, "Doctor Cooper."

Brent nodded and said, "She's ready for you, Doctor Patton."

"How was your hot date last night?"

"It was okay."

Doctor Patton recognized Brent wasn't acting in his usual positive manner. He put his hand on Brent's shoulder. "You alright?"

"Yeah, I'm good," he faked.

Doctor Patton lowered his head, "Brent. Come on, now. I know something's not right."

"You're right, Doc, but I'm okay and I don't want to discuss it right now."

"You were fine an hour ago in surgery."

Brent pleaded, "Doc!"

Doctor Patton put his hand in front of him and said, "Okay. How's Mrs. Collins?"

"She's ready for you," he said, then continued along the corridor.

Chapter 12

Slipped Away

Tuesday Midday (Rachel's Home Office)

Rachel's headset was small. The device went over her ear and had a thin boom microphone that reached to the edge of her mouth. Her hair was in a ponytail. She didn't have makeup on. There wasn't a reason to, since she worked from home. She wore dark gray leggings with a matching top, except that it wasn't as tight.

"Any new employees or terminations this week?" she said as she navigated the payroll system to the totals screen.

"Not this week, but I'll have one for you next time."

"Okay, do you have your totals ready?"

"Ready when you are."

"I have 240 regular hours, one and a half overtime hours, your reimbursement of thirty-six dollars and ninety-seven cents and Steve's commission at seven hundred sixty-two dollars."

"Did I say sixty-two? I meant ninety-two. Steve's commission should be seven hundred ninety-two dollars even."

"Oh, you probably said it right and my fat fingers hit the six instead of the nine. That's why we confirm totals."

Rachel went back to Steve's payroll record to make the change, then returned to the totals screen. "Okay, I got it now. It's showing seven hundred ninety-two dollars."

She unlocked her cell phone that was on her desk, but there weren't any new messages. When she advanced past the screen that showed totals for the current payroll, she confirmed their next appointment, "I'm showing our next payroll call is in two weeks from today. Does that work for you?"

"It sure does. Thank you, Rachel."

"You're welcome, Mrs. Morris. The courier will have those checks to you tomorrow before 5:00. What else can I do for you today?"

"That'll do it. Thanks again."

Rachel thanked Mrs. Morris again before she disconnected the call, then put a brief note in the system, NORMAL PAYROLL. TOTALS MATCHED.

She didn't have another payroll appointment until after lunch, but her lunch break didn't start until 12:30. She checked her cell phone again. Nothing. A different thought came to her mind. She pulled up her messages from the night before. One, she sent to Christine, her friend from Iowa, but she hadn't read it. She scrolled up to see the last exchange.

I have a date tonight.

Two hours later, Christine replied.

Get the fuck out of here.

Seriously. Can you believe it?

Tell me all about him.

I can't yet. I met him online. He's a
salesman.

Send me a picture when you can.

I will.

*You be safe. Don't go to his house.
Meet him at a common place. Don't
let him know what you drive. Don't
tell him where you live. Nothing. Got
it?*

Okay, Warden. LMAO!!!

*Send me a text when you get a
chance to let me know you're okay.*

I will.

That was at 10:03 Monday morning. The next message was from the night before when she was at the restaurant and sent one brief message.

I'm safe. He's hot. Chat later.

She scrolled a little more and saw the next messages she sent to Christine.

I'm home. Call when you can.

Forty-five minutes later, she sent one more message.

Where you at, hussy?

DELIVERED

Rachel changed from her chat with Christine to the one with Brent Cooper and read the last few messages, then accessed his contact card to edit the information. She changed his name to Doctor Brent Cooper and smiled when she saved it. She set her phone on her desk, then picked it up again. Without unlocking it, she placed it back on her desk, face down, then opened her appointment calendar in the payroll system, but only stared at it. She picked up her phone and sent another message to Doctor Brent Cooper.

I asked you a question, Doctor. Red
or White? If you don't tell me, I'll
bring something awful, then you'll
HAVE to tell me next time.

She watched the bottom corner of her computer screen at 4:59. It seemed to stay 4:59 for three minutes. When it finally changed to 5:00, she closed all the applications, then sent another message.

> Are we still on tonight? If so, what
> time? I'm going to get ready.

She finally received a reply.

> *Rachel, I am so sorry. I had a few*
> *things I needed to take care of. Bad*
> *day. I apologize. Yes, we're still on.*
> *What's your address and when should*
> *I pick you up?*

She started typing her address, then thought of Christine. What if something happened to her?

> I changed my mind. I'll meet you in
> the parking lot of the shopping
> center. I'll park near the street.
> There shouldn't be many people
> there. Is 7:00 too late?

The dots on the bottom of her screen flashed several times, then stopped, but flashed again before she received another message.

> *I think that's a good idea. 7:00 is*
> *perfect.*

She turned the light off in her office and closed the door when she walked out. That was her routine every day at 5:00 and was her method to ensure she didn't work outside of business hours. She walked to the sliding door in the living room at the back of her apartment. The rain was steady. It was darker than usual for that time of night, even on a rainy day. With the dining room light on, she could see her own reflection in the glass.

"Shit," she said aloud, not knowing if Brent planned to have dinner together or not. She figured if she asked, he might perceive it as a request, which it wasn't. She reached into her cabinet to get a paper plate, then another cabinet for white bread and finally the refrigerator for mustard and two slices of bologna. With the plate in her left hand and the sandwich in her right, she walked to her bedroom at the end of the hall and opened her closet. Balancing the sandwich and the plate in one hand, he pushed her softball uniform to the left, followed by several causal outfits. When she came across a low cut, white top, she pulled it out of her closet, put the sandwich on her dresser, took the shirt off the hanger and threw the skirt on her unmade bed. She stood in front of the mirror with the top held up to her chest. From behind the white top, she pulled the front of the dark gray shirt that she was wearing, down to match the cut of the white shirt, then pulled the white one away to look at herself in the mirror. The amount of cleavage showing was spot on. She smiled, bobbed her head from side to side, then threw the top on the bed to check the skirt that was on the same hanger. It was short; really short.

"I can't even bend over in this," she said, then returned to her closet. After flipping through a few more outfits, she came across a black night club dress that was long, similar to the one she wore the night before that was still draped

132

over her hamper. She got an appropriate reaction out of him when the dress fell over each side of her leg to reveal her thigh, but considered it was probably too formal for a night in, so she pushed it over and kept looking. A medium gray skirt was next. She pulled it out of the closet and held it up to her waist and judged herself in the mirror. She curled her lip, then threw the skirt onto the bed.

"What the hell am I doing?" she said, then went to her dresser, took a bite of the sandwich and opened her jeans drawer, thinking that if she wore jeans and a nice shirt, that was a balanced compromise between a fancy dress and her leggings. After all, she knew what she wore *underneath* was far more important. You know—just in case. She pulled out a pair of tight-fitting stretch jeans and the white, low-cut shirt she first laid on the bed.

She chuckled and said, "Now, for the fun part," and opened her underwear drawer. It didn't take long to decide on the white lace bra that brought the girls together nicely and a red thong. You know—just in case.

When she looked at the time, she blurted out, "Fuck!" and took a couple huge bites of her sandwich that filled her cheeks. She hurried to the bathroom on the other side of her bed and turned the water on in the shower. As she stripped, she threw her clothes across the room. Her leggings balled up and went straight into the hamper, but the top opened like a sail and fell short and onto the floor. She unfastened her bra, pulled her arms out, then took off her underwear and launched both into the hamper. She glanced over at her sandwich, walked around the bed, put the last bite into her mouth, and was still chewing when she entered the shower.

5:45 PM (The River House)

Brent pulled into the garage and closed the door before he turned off the Tacoma. The taillights darkened just before the door lowered and blocked them from John's view. John pulled up the security app.

"Shit, shit, SHIT!" he said as he sat on the floor. He put his head against the wall. His breathing became rapid. He looked up at the ceiling, then peeked out the window towards Dr. Cooper's house. It was still. He pulled up the app again, shook his head and whispered, "Fuck!" through gritted teeth.

SYSTEM: OFF (NOT RECOMMENDED)

John fumbled into the settings to reactivate the security system. With any luck, he could reset it before Brent entered the house. He selected the button for options and chose SYSTEM: ARMED (AWAY)

Inside the house, on the wall next to the stairs that led to the second floor, the security panel lit up, beeped twice and displayed the same status that John set.

From under the windowsill, he leaned until he could see Dr. Cooper's house with one eye. His heart beat fast and he exhaled slowly. The rain fell as steadily as the sound it made when the drops scattered on the roof of Charlie's house.

"What the hell is he doing?" John muttered when he looked at his phone. The security system was still armed. A minute later, the system status changed to OFF. He turned on the receiver for the microphones he emplaced, put the headphones on and listened. He couldn't monitor the security cameras. They were only operational when he armed the security system. The lights on the receiver showed which microphone was active when something in the house broke the silence. He closed his eyes and lowered his head.

Footsteps. Light footsteps gradually became louder. He opened his eyes long enough to see the light flashing next to Microphone 1. When the footsteps got louder, the sound changed to more of a shuffle. Click! More shuffling. He kept his eyes closed so his mind focused entirely on his sense of hearing. He heard a rattling sound, then the distinct sound of glass bottles clanging together lightly, then the quick burst of air that escaped the lid when Brent removed the bottle top. Next, he heard a slight slurp, a thud and a breathy, "Ah."

The sound that followed was loud enough to startle him. He threw the headphones into his lap and looked at the receiver again. The audio was still coming from Microphone 1. Even with the headphones in his lap, he heard the noise through them again. He looked out the window above him, but nothing had changed since the garage door closed. He put the headphones back on but heard nothing, then reflected on what he heard moments before.

The sound was brief, but loud. It sounded like something scraped or slid across a surface. A box, perhaps, that he slid across the bar in the dark area of the first floor where the microphone was. He glanced at the receiver several times, but all the lights were off, and no sound came through the headphones.

"Fucking batteries drained already?" he wondered out loud. He checked the security system again. It was still off. The lights on the receiver remained off for the next twenty minutes.

6:05 PM (Rachel)

Rachel rinsed her hair one more time, rinsed off all the soap, then turned the shower off. She dried her hair with the towel that hung on the bar just outside the shower, then wrapped it around her head. With a second towel, she dried her body, then checked the time on her cell phone. There wasn't enough time to dry her hair completely and straighten it, so she towel-dried it as much as she could, then put styling spray in her hair to show off her loose, natural curls. When she donned her white bra and red thongs, she stood in front of her mirror. She knew they should match but didn't have white thongs as sexy as the red ones, nor did she own a red bra as good as the white. She adjusted her breasts inside her bra until her cleavage was just right, then put her white shirt on to make sure the bra wasn't too visible through the shirt. Slightly visible was okay, but she didn't want to look trashy. She chose little makeup like the night before, but bold enough to wow him, particularly around her eyes. Before she slid into her jeans, she chose her best perfume. The scent that has gotten the most compliments in the past. A spray on her neck, one on her chest, then one on each wrist. She rubbed her wrists together, then wiped them across her abdomen.

6:20 PM (Doctor Cooper)

The shopping center was less than ten minutes away from the River House, so he had plenty of time. He went to the bar on the third floor and chilled four bottles of wine: two rosé and two white. He preferred dryer wines, but to be safe, he chose wines in the middle of the sweetness scale for Rachel. If she didn't like his choices, he had tonic water and top shelf gin readily available.

He entered the shower at 6:35 and was out by 6:40. His shoulder-length hair didn't take long to dry. He put on jeans, a white undershirt, a blue oxford and shiny black shoes over black socks. He stepped in front of his full-length mirror, straightened his belt buckle so the edge lined up with the seam of his zipper, added two sprays of cologne and left in the Z06.

The engine roared a throaty growl that John heard clearly from inside the Branson house. He even felt it. As he watched the Z06 dodge the deepest pits of Rivers Edge Lane, he thought about Dr. Cooper leaving the night before. He thought about the hide and go seek game Detective Fuller played with him. But as that bright yellow car drove into the distance, he thought mostly of Katie. He imagined her in the passenger side of Dr. Cooper's Corvette, looking back with fear in her eyes. Without making a sound, that look—just the look screamed, "Daddy, help me." His imagination replaced Brent with Fuller, who turned around and smiled at John, then his lips parted in a mischievous grin that seemed wider than his face. He threw his head back in laughter, then grabbed Katie's chin and forcefully turned it so she couldn't see her Daddy anymore.

He was cautious the previous night, and Dr. Cooper's house was vacant for three hours. With a glance towards the River House, he considered the opportunity he missed the night before. There was no way he would let it slip away again tonight.

Chapter 13

Unexpected Clue

Dr. Cooper pulled into a parking spot near the street with three minutes to spare. When he did, his phone vibrated.

RACHEL

6:57 PM

I'm on my way. I'm so sorry. Be there
in ten minutes.

He started typing, "I'm here and waiting," but didn't want to pressure her. He started again, "I'm in a parking spot near—" then deleted it. Finally, he sent, "No worries. See you soon."

Brent could see Rachel's car in the turn lane at the red light into the shopping center. Her's was second to the intersection. She tapped her hands on the steering wheel and glanced at her dashboard at least four times before the light turned green. When it did, the driver in front of her didn't go. She put both hands in the air and yelled something into the windshield with her neck stretched forward. Her hand hovered over the horn, but the driver in front of her rolled into the intersection before she pressed it. She followed closely behind until she turned off the access and into the first lane of the parking lot. Brent smiled. Rachel sped up, quickly engaged the brakes when she noticed his car only ten parking spaces away, then calmly turned into the parking place next to his. The rain was light.

He tried not to look but couldn't help himself from glancing out of the corner of his eye to watch her. She turned her car off and gathered her purse that was on the passenger seat and got out of the car. Brent lowered his window. Rachel stutter-stepped and approached him.

"Hi Rachel," he said with a grin.

She returned his greeting with a bigger smile, "Hi Brent."

"You can ride with me. I'll bring you back later, or you're welcome to follow me if it makes you feel more comfortable."

She fidgeted and started three different responses to dismiss the concern, but it didn't work.

"Here," he said. "Here's my driver's license. You can take a picture of it and send it to whoever you like and trust." He reached for his wallet.

His offer was enough to put her completely at ease. "That's not necessary," she said without looking at his identification, then walked around to the passenger side of the Z06 with her purse on her shoulder and a small umbrella in her hand. She tried not to show how excited she was, but had never been in a Corvette before. She also considered if she didn't express her excitement, it might send a message that she's been in plenty of Corvettes in her life and this one is no different from the others.

"Wow," She said. "Is this an airplane or a car? All the controls—it's awesome."

He pressed the brake and pushed the button to start it. Rachel said, "This thing sounds incredible."

"You a car fanatic?" he asked.

"Honestly, I don't know anything about them. Hell, I don't know anything about my Corolla either. Sorry if that bursts some ego bubble, but I just can't appreciate it as much as you probably do. It *is* badass, though. I can tell you that."

He backed out of the parking space and asked, "Have you eaten yet?"

"Yeah, I had a little—I'm fine."

"Let me ask differently. Are you hungry?"

"I can always eat, but you don't need to buy me dinner if you're not hungry."

He waited at the red light to pull out of the shopping center. Rachel noticed his grin, "What? What are you grinning at?"

"You're being difficult."

Her eyes opened widely, and she retorted, "I'm not being difficult? What are you talking about?"

"Do you like pizza?"

"Pizza's great."

"Then we'll get pizza."

He tried not to get caught when he glanced at her twice, then looked at her directly and said, "You look really nice tonight."

She blushed and looked away impulsively, bit her lips together to hide her smile, and said, "Thank you. You look good, too."

The light turned green, and he drove towards the restaurant. Rain fell harder and Brent changed the wipers from a delay to steady on.

(John Wolfe)

I waited five minutes to enter Brent's home again. The sun had set, but it wasn't completely dark yet. The rain favored my mission. There were fewer people on their decks, and there wasn't a single boat speeding along the Placid River. Another benefit was that Dr. Cooper forgot to arm his security system. I left my backpack under the window and only took my AR-15 that I slung across my back with the muzzle down, and gloves that I stuck into my back pockets. From the back of the Branson house, I put the hood up on my rain gear and looked in all directions to ensure no one could see me, then hurried to the wall behind the doctor's garage next to the door. I checked my perimeter again. Some porch lights were on across the river that still didn't rise significantly. At least, not yet. The rain had slowed but was falling more steadily again. With my gloves on, I turned to the door, picked the lock and entered his garage. Even with the two windows in the garage that faced the river, it was dark. I used the flashlight on my phone and investigated the garage. There were two long, metal shelves with storage bins on them to my right. I popped the lids on each of them. One was full of lint-free cloths, car wax, and damn near any other compound imaginable for detailing a vehicle. Another had Christmas lights and decorations. I don't know why, but Dr. Cooper didn't strike me as a man who would decorate his house for Christmas. The third one was half full of papers, photographs, and some little league trophies. I looked closer at the baseball trophy on top. The plaque showed FIRST PLACE, KING COUNTY, WA LITTLE LEAGUE 1985. I placed it back in the container, secured the lid, then looked around the rest of the garage, which was quite bare, except the Tacoma and the car with the tarp. I walked between the two, then towards the door into his house. To be completely certain, I checked the app one more time. SYSTEM: OFF (NOT RECOMMENDED)

I entered his house slowly and as quietly as I could, then walked straight across the game room to the bar. There was one beer top upside down on the bar. I looked at the shelves underneath. The microphone was still in place. I opened the small refrigerator. Two beer bottles that were in the door clanged together. I checked the top of the bar again. Nothing was on it. I crouched down so my eyes were even with the bar and shined the light of my phone towards me but saw no scrapes or scratches. The top was smooth. I looked around me and wondered what the fuck could have made that loud scraping sound, then noticed the octagon card table. The top of that was also smooth, but not as smooth as the bar. I grasped the edges of the wooden top, lifted, then pulled it so it dragged across the table. It didn't sound any louder than wood scraping on wood. Maybe the microphone magnified the sound when I heard it, but the pitch seemed different. It wasn't as deep of a sound as I heard through the receiver only an hour before. I ran my gloves along the walls. The sound of leather on drywall wasn't nearly as loud, and the pitch was even higher than the card table. I returned the wooden top of the card table. That sound was deeper and louder than when I dragged it off, but still didn't seem to match what I heard. I walked up to the empty wall. The dark one behind the bar. There was nothing in front of it and it sounded the same as the other walls when I dragged my gloves across it, so I went upstairs and hoped to find a box sitting around somewhere. Based on the sound, it would be a heavy box; I was sure of that. Maybe I was looking for a wooden box instead of cardboard. When I got to the second floor, I looked in the kitchen, living room and dining area. There was nothing there that wasn't earlier that day. The hallway to his bedroom seemed longer in the dark than it was early that morning. I opened each door until I reached his bedroom. Nothing. Fucking nothing.

I started back down the stairs, ready to dismiss the sound as some weird interference or static, but at the first step, I stopped, backed up and continued to the third floor. I checked the microphone between the wall and the refrigerator. It was in the same place I put it, so I stood in his entertainment room, but stayed away from all the windows that faced the front of the house. His theater seating was as impressive as I've ever seen.

The more I studied this case, the more I questioned who was really dumping girls into the Placid River. It was Tuesday and weather warning continued through late Thursday. The bodies of all the women that surfaced were in a state of decomposition, which takes a couple of days, at least. If the killer was going to strike again and Chief Merritt could expect another body to surface at the amphitheater, the girl was probably already dead and being held underwater. I never pretended to be a detective. That shit requires too much thinking. It was becoming clear that wherever the killer was, perhaps a little farther upstream, it was already too late.

Each mission assigned to me lasted a few days, at most. All except this one. When I was here in the Spring, Sam kept me on the case longer than any other. I needed an end. I had to know how long this case would hold me up before I could return to Indianapolis to find—and kill Detective Fuller. I'm also not a fucking idiot. There's enough sense in my brain to know that I had already pushed my limits with Sam and wasn't about to ask him any more questions.

Standing there, in that huge, open room, I imagined what I would do to Fuller when I found him. Would I kill him fast to get it over with and finally reach some level of peace with my daughter's death? Some type of closure? Is that too much to ask for? Or would I kill him slowly and remind him with every action of how he tortured my sweet girl? What would *you* do in that situation? I guess it's like finding your wife with another man. You don't really know what you'd do unless you've been in the situation yourself. I've heard of people shooting both of them. I've heard of people killing one or the other. Hell, I've even heard of one man who listened to the other man's story and sided with him, filed for divorce and it was over. What would you do? What will I do when given the chance?

I peeked around the edge of the window towards Rivers Edge Lane. Dr. Cooper really built in a great location. The view from the third floor was peaceful. Although it was only three floors, it seemed larger than that. A high rise looking over one and two-story homes.

Before I left, I went into the kitchen on that floor. I looked out the window at the tree line with the Placid on the other side. I was just about to walk

144

downstairs when I noticed something on the counter. Four bottles of wine chilling in a metal container. Two whites and two rosés. The realization of the situation occurred to me about a minute too late. Headlights bounced into the large wall of windows. I knew in my gut who it was but had to look for myself. I ran to the edge of the window and peeked around to see. Just as I thought, Dr. Cooper was home and less than a hundred yards away from his house.

I ran down the stairs to the landing and started down the next steps towards the second floor. Halfway down, I heard the garage door opening. I froze, took a few steps up, then stopped and evaluated if it would be faster to run out the door off the main kitchen on the second floor. I ran down again. The garage door stopped. I didn't know how much time I had and wasn't certain there was an exit to the back on the second floor. I skipped every other step when I ascended to the third floor, ran to the back of the house, unlocked one of the French doors to the deck, exited, then closed it.

I listened closely. The roaring engine was still running, so I took my chance and ran as fast as I could down the wet wooden deck stairs to the second level, turned to the next set of stairs and ran again to the ground, next to the door that accessed the garage.

He turned the engine off. The door closed. I squinted my eyes in confusion when I heard a second door close. The headlights shone through the door for a moment, then turned off. I stood as still as I could, but my breathing sounded like I ran a marathon. I was certain they heard me. My heart beat fast and loud as I cautiously leaned my shoulder against the cinderblock wall, so the muzzle of my rifle didn't scrape on the brick. I heard muffled laughter inside the garage. When the main bay door closed, I ducked under the window as much as I could and ran back to the Branson house. Just as I cleared the dark brown house next to Charlie's, I felt a blow from my right side.

I felt arms around me. My feet lifted off the ground, and I launched five feet into the street. It was a tackle that would have impressed any professional team. He threw my hood back as he straddled me, relaxed and said, "Goddammit, John."

"Hi Chief," was all I could say. Todd got off me and offered his hand, which I gladly took since I didn't know the extent of my pain. When I stood, we both glanced towards the River House, then ran to the back of Charlie's old place and entered through the back.

I asked Todd, "What the fuck are you doing?"

"My job, John. I'm doing my job. I didn't know it was you. Didn't recognize you with the hood up. What's going on next door?"

"I'm not sure," I started. I gave him every detail of my adventure as I recalled it.

"Who's the other person with him?" he asked.

"I don't know. I can't be sure there *was* another person. Two doors closed, but he could have walked around to the passenger side and gotten something off the seats."

"What about the laughter? Was there one person or two?"

"Man, it sounded like two, but if he was on the phone, it could have been someone I heard he was on the phone with."

I removed my rain gear, placed my rifle against the wall, then peered out the window to Dr. Cooper's house.

"Chief," I started.

"Yeah."

"What if it's too late? You said you found all the women partially decomposed, so they were under the water for at least a couple days. If he—or she—kills again, the girl might already be dead."

"I know that. That's why I'm out here."

He took his head cover off and ran his fingers through his hair. "I've become so involved in this case—obsessed. I have to stop this."

"What if it's not Cooper? What if whoever is doing this knows you're onto someone else and is using a specific place in the river to dump the bodies so you keep suspecting Cooper? Chief, they could come from anywhere along the river, bringing their partially decayed victims here and dumping them."

Chief Merritt was silent for a minute. "Any ideas?"

"The tree line behind the house. Set up one of your people in the open field on the East side of Brent's place, against the trees or even *in* the tree line."

"You really don't think it's Doctor Cooper?"

I shrugged my shoulders. "It's hard to say, man. If it's him, he's damn good. I can't find any access point to dump the victims, so if it's him, he has to be taking them down the bank. If they're dead before he dumps them, I don't know. I just can't imagine, with as much publicity as this case has, that people aren't watching the river all night, waiting for a body to float by after it's been raining or to see the killer dump the bodies. It's what people do. Like the goddamn web sleuths that have good intent but can fuck up a case with speculation and conspiracy."

Todd didn't interrupt.

"Chief, I'm not saying you're tracking the wrong guy. Just don't narrow your suspects down to this one dude."

"Why do you give a shit anyway, John?"

"I have to get the fuck out of here and back to Indianapolis."

Todd sighed, looked at the ceiling and shook his head. He put his cover back on his head and walked towards the door. Before he left, he turned around, "You okay?"

"Yeah, I'm alright," I said.

"You said you found a box in the garage. Anything of value in it?"

"Car wax and shit, Christmas decorations and an old memory box."

"A memory box? What's in it?"

"Old certificates, little league stuff from Washington." I thought of Katie in the Girl Scouts when she was little and smiled. Somehow her memory made Dr. Cooper more of a person than a case. "He was on a first-place team in 1985. King County, WA."

I pictured Katie in her uniform with one badge on her sash.

"What did you say?" Merritt asked somberly.

"First place baseball team."

"When and where?" Todd demanded.

"King County, WA. 1985."

"The Green River," he muttered, then hurried out the door.

Chapter 14

Attraction

Rachel broke the silence on the way to the restaurant, "You said you had a bad day. What happened?"

"Is that what I said?"

She said, "Yeah, it was after I asked if we were still on tonight." She looked at her phone and read, "Rachel, I am so sorry. I had a few things I needed to take care of. Bad day. I apologize. Yes, we're still on. What's your address and when should I pick you up?"

Brent faked a smile, "I guess I did say that—just a nasty patient. It happens sometimes. It's a condition called post-operative delirium and effects people differently. The lady I had today was really mean after surgery and—well, let's just say—she recognizes her mistake. I've seen it before plenty of times, but I've never had someone hit me."

Rachel gasped, "She *hit* you?"

Brent snickered, "Yeah. Clocked me in the jaw before I even realized what was happening."

"What did you do?"

"I stepped out of the room and washed my face to cool off." He shook his head and said, "Jesus, I haven't been hit like that since—" He sighed, and his smile faded. "in a long time."

"You said you were from Portland. How long did you live there?"

"Seattle."

"Whatever."

"I moved there after I graduated Med School."

"Where did you go?"

"U of W. University of Washington in Seattle."

"Jeez, how long did you go through Doctor School?"

Brent laughed, "Too fucking long. About twelve years."

"Holy shit. I can't imagine."

"That includes school, residency, continuing education, boards and any other clown show circus bullshit they can make you go through. What about you? Did you go to college?"

"The University of Life," she laughed.

"Well, you're much smarter than I am then. Being a doctor, we kind of feel like we miss out on life sometimes. We go from High School to becoming professional students, then rush into our career. That *is* our life."

"Did you ever want more?"

"Hold that thought. Here's the restaurant."

He pulled into the carry out space near the doors of the restaurant. She didn't know whether she should get out herself or wait for him to open her door for her. Waiting wasn't her style, so she opened the door then extended her umbrella above the car.

"Hang on there," Brent said, then hurried around the car with his head down to protect himself from the steady rain. He reached the passenger side, took the umbrella from Rachel and held it for her as she exited. The rain was loud when they huddled under the small umbrella and rushed to the door.

An employee greeted them from behind the counter loudly above the noise of music playing. "Hey guys. You dining in, or taking it with you?"

Brent glanced at Rachel, then looked out the door at the rain. "Carry out, please," then told Rachel, "This place is fast."

"My name's Justin. What'll you have tonight?"

Brent asked Rachel, "What do you typically order?"

"I'm simple. I get pepperoni and extra cheese, but you can get whatever you want."

Brent told Justin, "Large pepperoni with extra cheese, please."

"What type of crust?"

Brent fumbled over his response when he said, "Uh—regular, I guess," then looked for confirmation.

Rachel smiled and said, "Hand tossed is fine."

"See what I mean? The University of Life taught you more than twelve years of school taught me."

Justin rang up the order and said, "We have one coming out of the oven in about three minutes."

"Wow," Rachel exclaimed, "they *are* fast."

After they turned down the options Justin offered them, like breadsticks, drinks, cookie dough, cinnamon bread, cheesy bread and damn near everything else on their menu, he completed the order, and another employee brought the box to the counter. Brent paid, balanced the pizza in one hand and pushed the release on the umbrella with his other hand just outside the door. He handed her the pizza, opened the car door for her while holding the umbrella, closed it to hand back to her, then hurried around the back of the car to the driver's side.

"How long is this rain supposed to last?" he asked.

"All day tomorrow and Thursday. It's supposed to stop late on Thursday."

"Hmm," he replied when he started the car.

He backed out of the parking lot and onto River Road. When he reached the top of the hill at the entrance to Rivers Edge Lane, he engaged his left turn signal and waited for one oncoming car.

"Is there even a road there?" Rachel asked.

Brent smiled and said, "I guess we'll find out."

When the car passed, Rachel said, "That is not an appropriate response, Doctor Brent—Oh!" she interrupted herself when the front of the car pointed down the steep hill.

Brent slowed the car to a crawl. The pitted road jostled them as they crept along it.

"Don't they pave this? Rachel asked.

"No, it's a flood plain. Mount Placid doesn't want to deal with it, so all of us kind of live here at our own risk."

"It's kind of creepy back here."

"I thought the same thing when I first moved here. In the front here, people don't take good care of their property."

Rachel looked around at what she could see, which wasn't much. Some properties looked as though the owners missed a few appointments with a junkyard. "You do live back here, right?" she asked jokingly.

"Yes, I'm the highest point at the end of the road, right against the river."

When they passed Ted Johnson's place, the headlights shined on the front of his house.

"Holy shit," Rachel said. "Looks totally out of place. I love it. Nobody would ever guess there's a place like this back here."

Brent glanced to his left, between Charlie Branson's old house and the brown two-story next to it. Rachel noticed and said, "What is it?"

He pressed the button to open his garage door and said, "I thought I saw someone in the back between those two houses."

He pulled straight in and turned the car off. The headlights stayed on, as they usually did, for a minute. Rachel opened her own door and got out. Brent closed his door. Rachel closed hers, noticed the two other vehicles and said, "Who else lives here?"

Brent chuckled, "Just me."

The headlights went out, and he led her into the house.

"Shit," he said. "I forgot to arm the security before I left."

"It's a small town, Brent. Nothing ever happens in a small town."

He thought about the murders and being questioned—even blamed for the victims showing up in the water but didn't bring attention to it. Maybe it was better that Rachel didn't know about the dead girls.

"I had the security system installed during construction. No place safer that I know of."

"I guess with a place like this, I'd want to protect it, too."

"Ready for the grand tour?" he asked when he took the pizza from Rachel.

Brent was uniquely humble, but also felt pride in showing her around his house.

"This is my game room."

"It's perfect."

"I'll show you more later, but right now, I'm hungry. Want to see upstairs?"

"After you, sir."

Brent led her up the stairs to the second floor, turned to climb the next set of steps and said, "That's my main floor. I'll show you that later, too."

When they reached the top floor in the entertainment area, Brent called out into the air, "Virginia, turn on the third-floor lights at thirty percent."

Rachel watched recessed lights around the edges of the ceiling glow. "Holy shit. Look at that theater setup."

A female voice spoke through unseen speakers, "Is that the setting you requested, Mister Cooper?"

"Yes, Virginia. Thank you."

"You're welcome, Mister Cooper. I'll be here if you need anything else."

He asked Rachel, "You like it?"

"It's incredible."

"I enjoy it, but it's the dumbest thing I did to this house."

"Why?"

"The second floor living room underneath us has fewer windows. I should have had them install the theater downstairs instead."

"I think it's amazing. And it's so cool, you have one of those virtual assistants."

He told Rachel, "Yeah, she's my robot. She's the only human voice I hear most days." He turned to her and shook his head. "Shit, she's not even human." He continued into the large kitchen, "Sometimes I tell her to talk to me and she asks if I want her to read a story to me. You'd be amazed at some shit people write." He laughed. "I look at my phone sometimes and ask Virginia to call someone. It doesn't work. The robot in my phone has a different name. Never thought I'd live long enough to get my robots confused."

Rachel laughed at his comment but wasn't paying much attention to him. Instead, she was taking in the atmosphere of Brent's house. Part of her wondered what she was doing. She's out of her league. She'd never been on a date with anyone like him. Certainly not a doctor, that she knew of. She questioned many things in her mind. What if he's just being nice? Was she being fake for him or comfortable enough to show her genuineness? She wasn't trying hard to be someone she wasn't. What if she gets close to him and he leaves her because she's just not like him? *Jesus, Rachel*, she thought. *It's a date. Turn it off, lady.*

Brent opened the pizza box on the counter and reached for a bottle of red wine.

"The beverage is fancier than the meal, but we can pair the two together."
He looked at the label of the bottle. "I probably should have gotten a cabernet
out, but they're a bit dry. I wasn't sure if you like dry or sweet."

"Come to think of it," then she annunciated, "Doctor—Brent—Cooper. I
don't know what you like either since you didn't reply to me this afternoon.
That's why I didn't bring any," which was a little white lie. In reality, she ran
out of time.

"I know. I'm sorry. It wasn't on purpose," he said sincerely.

She touched his arm and said softly, "Hey, it's all good. I'm just messing
with you."

He smiled and said, "Thanks" then got paper plates out of the cabinet and
tore paper towels off the stainless-steel holder on the counter. When he handed
it to her, he announced, "Your fine dining ware, Miss—Oh, Hell. Um, Miss—
why the Hell can't I remember your last name?"

"Because it's not on the dating site. I marked my last name as private so it
wouldn't show. I'm leery of those sites. You never know if you're meeting a
nice guy or some murderous lunatic that would as soon hack me up as he would
take me out to dinner."

"If it's any consolation, Rachel, I'm not going to hack you up," he smiled.

"Good. That's comforting," she joked. "If you ever felt the urge to, I
humbly request you just break up with me or tell me we can't date anymore.
There's no need for slicing and hacking and stabbing."

Brent laughed, "Wait, I said nothing about stabbing. I just said I wouldn't
hack you up."

Rachel laughed harder, "No stabbing either, okay?"

Brent mocked disappointment with laughter and a sigh, then said, "Okay. I guess."

When they each served themselves, he offered to sit out on the third-floor balcony.

"Did it stop raining?" Rachel asked.

"It's covered. We'll stay dry," Brent replied and turned the lock on the French door. He stopped and looked at the handle. "That's weird," he said as he inspected it. "I never unlock this door."

"Like you never leave your alarm system unarmed?" Rachel teased.

"Yeah, yeah, yeah—whatever," he laughed when he held the door open for her.

Whey they settled and started eating, Rachel said, "Just before we pulled into the restaurant, you were talking about living in Portland. I think you were talking about life as a student and doctor."

"Oh, yeah—you mean the lack of life outside of being a doctor."

"OH!" Rachel blurted. "I remember. I asked if you ever wanted more out of life than the education, then jumped right into your career."

Brent sipped his wine. "I never really thought about it much. I'm not the kind of guy who wishes for something different for himself. I chose my path, and any rewards or consequences are mine alone. There are times I wish I chose differently. I grew up eating pancakes for most meals. Sometimes, dinner was a couple pieces of toast with butter and syrup. Dad said it was no different than pancakes. Not because he was trying to trick me." Brent smiled. "He was a positive man." Brent pointed to Rachel and impersonated his father,

"Son, work for what you need. Pray for what you want. Enjoy the things you have and never WISH for something different."

Rachel smiled, "Is that what he used to say?"

"He said it. He lived it. I used to hate him for saying that to me all the time. It wasn't until I got older that I understood what he meant." He looked into the trees beyond the roof of the balcony. Rachel didn't interrupt his thoughts. He continued, "I swore on my life I would never live a day of my life like I did as a kid."

"You mentioned your Mom at dinner last night. Is she still around?"

"No. She—um—" He looked at Rachel again. "She died. I had just turned sixteen. They got into a fight. She was drunk again and came after him. They fought all the time. But not after that night. That was the last time she opened his head up. He—yeah—uh, that's that, I guess."

Rachel reached her hand out and touched Brent's. "I'm sorry."

"It's all good. I'm fine. That was a long time ago. She had it coming to her, anyway. If he didn't do it that night, I would have." He looked into Rachel's eyes, "I promise you that." He sipped his wine and said, "I would have, and believe me, I wouldn't have wished for something different either."

Rachel put her pizza on her paper plate and sipped her wine. She didn't know how to respond. Brent shook his head, smiled and said, "Enough of that shit. What about you? You still in touch with your parents?"

"Before I get into that, can I ask you something?"

"Sure."

"What happened to your Dad after that?"

158

"He's still in Portland. She was still alive when the police showed up, and she blamed him for attacking her. What started as probably a few nights in jail and a lengthy investigation turned into a murder charge when she died. I was Dad's only defense, and as a kid, nobody gave a shit about my side. She was my stepmom and I hated her. I tried to tell them everything I could to make them believe she was an awful human being, and it only made me sound like a bitter kid who loved his dad and hated his stepmom. The neighbors took me in for a few days. When the police came back, the officer took his hat off, and said, 'Your mom's not coming home, son.'"

Brent smiled, then started laughing. "It was the best news I had ever heard. I asked the officer if he was sure. He nodded and told me he was. I laughed, thanked him, then went to bed."

"You laughed?"

"Fuck yeah, I laughed. It was over. The beatings were over. The drunken rage was over. Blaming me for everything was over. I saw a shrink for a while. More because of my reaction to the news than it was that I was a troubled kid. I kept my grades up. School was easy for me. It was kind of boring at times. I stayed with the neighbors until I turned eighteen. They were great. I've called a few times throughout the years to catch up. They even came to my graduation from Med School. That was the last time I talked to them."

Rachel listened for more, and Brent continued, "Not for any particular reason. I just haven't called them in a while but fuck it. The phone works both ways." He stood and said, "I'm getting another piece. Do you want one?"

"Yes, please."

He brought out the box and the bottle of wine, then filled both of their glasses. "Enough about me. Really. I'm not discussing me anymore. What about you? Tell me about the life of Rachel."

"Not much to tell, I guess. I had a pretty good childhood. High school was great. I was an average student, then started working after graduation. I worked a couple of odd jobs before starting with the payroll company I work for now."

"Odd jobs, like what?"

"I waited tables."

"Where?"

Rachel grinned and said, "Buffalo Bill's."

"Oh, with the tight shirts that don't cover your stomach?"

"That's the one."

Brent sipped his wine, leaned back with a smile and said, "I could see that."

Shyly, Rachel took a bite of her pizza, but found the courage to pull her shoulders back and say, "The girls got me some decent tips back in the day, but can we talk about something other than my boobs?"

"Like what?"

"How did you find this place and why did you move away from Portland?"

"Seattle."

Rachel was feeling the effects of the wine. She still had pizza in her mouth when she said, "Whatever."

"I moved because Mount Placid looked like a nice place. I had a friend of mine in Seattle who was going to another school for architecture. He designed it based on my specifications and demands. I bought three lots here, tore it all down and built my own place."

"What attracted you to Mount Placid?"

Brent looked beyond the porch and into the trees, then focused on the river behind Rachel. All expression faded from his face when he reflected, "Small town. Secluded property." He sipped his wine and said, "The River."

Chapter 15

Want to Play a Game?

The rain fell steadily. There was one corner of the River House—just one that was blanketed in darkness. The Northeast corner, which was farthest from Charlie Branson's place, was the only location around the perimeter of Dr. Cooper's house that no artificial light from the nearby houses or streetlights reached.

I shed my rain gear inside the Branson House when I heard the couple casually discussing murderous lunatics. I kept hearing Brent in my mind. *If it's any consolation, Rachel, I'm not going to hack you up.* Visions of Katie flashed in my mind as I recalled when Dr. Cooper stated he didn't say anything about stabbing.

I was back in the Coroner's office. My daughter's body lied on a cold metal table inside a white zippered bag. Her face was mangled. Her lips split open. Her teeth were knocked out. Her hair was tangled with sticks and leaves. Her red shirt was unbuttoned. Dried blood ran from six stab wounds in her stomach.

I forced myself to envision her smile the last time I saw her alive. With the tattered photo in my hand, I could hear her, *I love you Daddy.*

Although Dr. Cooper's words were merely circumstantial, there were far too many incriminating events. Many of which, he described freely in great detail to Rachel. Here's this kid, sixteen years old, who finds out his Dad killed his Stepmother, and what did he do? The motherfucker laughed. He laughed and went to bed. I didn't know the connection Chief Merritt made when he mentioned the Green River after I told him about the trophy, but based on his expression, I don't think it was in Dr. Cooper's favor.

What attracted you to Mount Placid?

Secluded Property. The river.

I suddenly felt like I approached the situation from the wrong angle. What if it's not him? I reflected on every case assigned to me in the past. I never gave the benefit of the doubt. This one was different. I spent time here in the Spring. Dead girls surfaced while I watched the subject. Does that mean he's innocent? The truth is it was a failure of imagination. What if Dr. Brent Cooper *was* a murderous lunatic?

My clothes were soaked and heavy, but rain that falls on vinyl is much louder than when it falls on cloth. I looked at Katie's picture again before I returned it to my pocket. What if it was me? What if I snatched Detective Fuller and brought him to my elaborate river house at the end of Rivers Edge Lane? What would I do to him? Where would I do it? Above all, how would I get away with it time after time? Trust me, if it was possible to kill a man more than once, I would spend the rest of my goddamn life taking great pleasure in killing Fuller again—and again.

I sat comfortably on the wet ground and listened.

"So, you like river life." Rachel stated.

Brent's response was cheery, "I'll take you out in my boat sometime."

Rachel smiled, "I'd like that."

Brent pointed at the pizza box, "You want more?"

She leaned back and sighed, "No, thank you. I've had plenty. I could use a refill, though."

"As you wish."

I thought of ways I could get her away from him. If I ran up the stairs, I'd scare the shit out of her. If I whispered loudly, and she looked down, she'd think I'm some homeless dude and would undoubtedly rush inside to tell Dr. Cooper there was a man under his deck. I thought of specifically what I could whisper to get her attention and have her trust me quickly. I could step away from under the deck and to the edge of the tree line, then say, "Rachel, please be very quiet. I'm just off the deck in front of you," then I could tell her she has to get away from him. In each scenario, I had to imagine myself as Rachel. Who would I trust more? The guy pouring wine for me in a three-story fancy house or the drenched man whispering loudly to her from under the deck?

"Here you go," Brent said.

Rachel became mesmerized. The rain pounded the leaves of the trees in front of her, and she said, "I could sit out here forever. I love the sound of rain and storms." She stretched her neck from side to side. Brent stood behind her, sipped his wine and set the glass on the table. He gently guided her hair to her back, then placed his hands on her shoulders. With only his fingertips, he rubbed both sides of her neck. She bowed her head, dropped her shoulders and whispered, "Why do I feel so connected to you?"

He whispered back, "Maybe because I'm touching you. We're literally connected right now."

She laughed, pulled her hand up and slapped his hand playfully. He traced her jawbone from her ears. She leaned her head back. His fingertips met at her chin. He extended his fingers entirely. With his thumbs on the edge of her jawbone, he rotated his hands, so his fingers surrounded her neck with the tips barely touching in the front. She moaned.

"You ready for that tour of the house?" he asked into her ear.

She nodded.

Two stories down, I couldn't hear them over the sound of the rain. A full minute of silence passed, then they went inside. When the door closed on the third floor, I rushed across the soggy ground under the deck to the door into the garage. Would he start on the third floor? It was mostly open. A tour of the third floor wouldn't take long. Maybe he'll skim the third floor, then go down to the second. The kitchen, bedrooms and main living area were on the second floor, which would take the longest to show her around. Where would they settle? The game room? His bedroom? If I was a betting man, I'd go all in on the game room with the bar.

I crouched upon the ground and put my head down to gather my thoughts. I'm not me. I'm not here on a mission to take out a serial killer.

I sighed.

I'm here to woo a lady. I'm a wealthy doctor on a date with an attractive girl. I want to kiss her. I want to take advantage her. I want to kill her—and get away with it.

The bar. Definitely the bar. There would be puddles of water everywhere if I went inside at that moment, so I ran as fast as I could to Charlie's house. I stripped bare in the kitchen, dried myself with the towel and put on dry clothes and shoes. Under the window in the living room, I turned the receiver on and listened through the headphones.

"These are spare rooms for someday. Right now, they're mostly empty."

"Someday?"

"Someday if I decide I want something more, I guess."

"Wow, the rooms are enormous."

"This is the Master Bedroom."

Rachel chuckled and said, "And you're the master."

Brent's face turned red. Rachel gasped and said, "Oh, my God. Is Doctor Brent Cooper embarrassed?

"Stop," he said playfully. "You're making it worse."

"Wow. I love this room. You have your bed on a pedestal."

Brent called out, "Virginia, turn on bedroom."

Rope lights around the pedestal slowly dimmed on, and the virtual assistant confirmed it did what Brent had asked it to do.

"That's kind of romantic," Rachel said, then placed her hand around Dr. Cooper's arm. He looked at his arm and she pulled her hand away. "I'm sorry. Oh, the wine."

Dr. Cooper faced her and smiled. Rachel turned her back to the wall and looked into his eyes. He reached his left hand between her hair and her neck, then leaned towards her. She licked her lips seductively and bit her bottom lip when she leaned towards him.

Brent whispered, "Is it too soon?"

She grabbed the back of his neck firmly, pulled him towards her and muttered, "Shut up."

Their kiss was passionate, but brief. Both pulled away, smiling. Brent took a deep breath and exhaled through pursed lips, then called out, "Virginia, turn off bedroom." He took her hand and led her to the first floor.

When they entered the game room, he turned the light on with the switch next to the front door. Rachel comfortably walked into the game room. Brent stayed by the front door and watched her walk away. He focused on her tight jeans, rested his elbow on his other arm, then touched the edge of his lips with his thumb.

"Want to play a game?" he asked.

I peered out the window, which wasn't at all beneficial. I still couldn't see inside the house. Why didn't I emplace my own cameras? Why didn't I consider he wouldn't arm the security system while he was home? Those security cameras were my eyes, and I was blind. I heard Dr. Cooper impersonating his father. *Work for what you need, pray for what you want, and don't wish for something different.* I needed to get inside that house! I didn't know how, and I didn't know when, but I had to get in there. It might have been the only opportunity I had. With the security system unarmed, I could move around his house without being seen by the cameras. *Don't wish for something different.* I looked up to the ceiling and mouthed, "Please don't let me be too late."

The sound of the rain on the roof got louder. I guess it was God's way of telling me to fuck off. Why couldn't he spend time with her on the second or third floor? Because there were no windows on the first, that's why.

"What kind of game," Rachel asked.

"The kind that there's no way in Hell you can beat me."

"Oh, really now?" she flirted.

"Yes, really."

She sauntered to the pool table and leaned on it. Her back arched in a way that showed off her curves perfectly. "Let me see here," she delayed, then walked to the end of the pool table opposite Brent. She leaned over the table as if she was holding a pool cue and smirked at him. Her shirt sagged, showing off a little of her white, lacy bra and a lot of her cleavage. "A nice game of pool, Doctor Brent Cooper? Hope I don't distract you." She stood straight and said, "Because if you got distracted, I just might win."

Brent walked towards her slowly. She held up her finger and said, "Stop," then strutted to the dartboard on the wall as if she were on a catwalk. "Maybe darts are a better choice. I don't play much, but I've heard it's all about the tip and getting your dart right in the middle."

Dr. Cooper clenched his fists.

Rachel walked towards the octagon table, "Perhaps a special game of poker is more up your alley."

She ran her fingertips along the cover of the table, then walked towards Brent the same way she walked towards the dart board. She stood toe to toe with him and grinned. "Surely, there's one of those that—how did you put it?" She leaned towards him and kissed him once. "Oh, yeah, there's no way in Hell I can beat you."

"Rachel," he whispered.

"Yes?"

"This isn't why I brought you here."

"This isn't why I came, either, but here we are." She kissed him again.

That time, they kissed much longer. Dr. Cooper's fists relaxed, and he grabbed Rachel's shoulders. Their heads tilted from side to side. Their tongues wrestled. When they stopped to catch their breath, Brent said, "This isn't me, Rachel."

She unbuttoned the top of his oxford. "It isn't me, either. I swear it. I just feel so connected to you," she said, then unbuttoned the next.

They kissed again, somehow even more passionately. As fast as Rachel unbuttoned Brent's shirt, Dr. Cooper unbuttoned hers. When he reached the last one, he threw the white shirt off her shoulders and she let it fall to the floor. He untucked his oxford just in time for Rachel to access the last button. He dropped his shirt to the floor, then pulled his undershirt over his head and let it fall. His kisses strayed from her mouth. He reached his hand behind her back, and under her hair. He kissed her ear and her collarbone, then grabbed her neck.

"What the fuck is she thinking?" I said out loud. I couldn't believe what I heard. The alcohol and passionate attraction made her vulnerable, as much as it did him. I quickly put on my rain gear, then pulled away the corner of the carpet in the living room to hide my rifle. I reached into the other main pocket of my backpack, retrieved my .45 and three cameras, tucked the pistol into the back waistline, then ran to the back of the River House.

Before I went inside, I walked to the edge of the water, near Dr. Cooper's floating dock. The river was rising. The water flowed strongly. As the dock rose and fell with the current, the empty barrels made a slapping sound under the dock. Dr. Cooper's boat swayed. It was only a matter of time. I knew Chief Merritt wasn't far away, but he was good. I looked up and down the banks of the river but couldn't see him. At that moment, I considered Chief Merritt would make a great addition as an agent, like me.

I hurried to the wall behind the house and under the deck to consider my entry point. With the two inside preoccupied, I slowly climbed to the highest deck. Under the protection from the rain, I hid my rain gear in the corner behind the hot tub, then dried my shoes the best I could. I reached my hand to my waist on my back and drew my .45. With my back against the wall, I peeked into the window of the french door, then slowly turned the handle. My heart jumped when the door squeaked. I froze. With the door open only an inch, I leaned my ear to listen. The insulation that made his house so quiet

170

became my protection. I opened the door farther, and the door didn't make a sound. I squeezed inside, turned the handle and pushed until the door rested against the jamb, then slowly released the handle.

At the top of the stairs, I listened, but heard nothing. I pointed my pistol down the space in the banister that was unobstructed all the way to the first floor. When I relaxed the pistol, I looked around the entertainment room, then took one step at a time, toe first, then heel. I stopped to listen at each step. No talking. No kissing. No heavy breathing. No moans or giggles. I reached the landing and peeked down the next set of steps and into the kitchen. Carefully balancing my weight with each step, I approached the banister and pointed the .45 down. Seeing nothing, I crouched on the floor of the landing so I could see all the way into the kitchen and part of the living room. *Where the hell did they go?*

I eased myself step by step down to the base of the second floor and peered down the hallway to the double doors of the Master Bedroom. The doors were closed.

My eyes darted from the hallway to the kitchen, down the stairs, into the living room and back again.

Her voice was muffled when she said, "Brent, I can't." I looked down the hallway at the closed bedroom doors.

He sighed, "Okay—okay," he said, then took a deep breath. I hurried down the stairs and into the game room. His oxford, white undershirt and jeans were in one pile and her white top and jeans were in another. The doors opened, and he asked, "I'm getting another glass of wine, do you want one?"

171

I hid in the nook behind the wall near the back in the opposite corner from the bar and stayed there until he ran up the stairs.

"No, thank you. I better make you take me home."

"Oh, come on. One more?"

I heard the glub—glub of the wine when he poured it into the glasses and he called out, "I promise, it will be the best glass of wine you've ever had in your life."

Chapter 16

The Wall

I stayed behind the wall in the corner and listened to them giggling playfully upstairs. The air conditioner turned on and created a white noise to masque sound of my movement. It was dark in the corner, but the few lights that were on lit up the dark corner enough for me to find a place to put the first camera. I stuck it high on the dark wall so I could see most of the game room. All except the entrance and the front door. The door to the master bedroom was still open, and neither Brent nor Rachel showed signs they would honor Rachel's request to go home.

Although it was muffled, I heard them talking upstairs. Rachel asked, "You're not mad at me, are you?"

"Jesus, why would I be mad?"

"Because I'm not ready for—that."

"Oh, God, no. I'm not mad at all. How could I be? We're both relaxed and did just about everything two people *can* do other than *that*."

"Good," she replied.

"You listen," he started. "I don't care if it's me or anyone else in your future. If you say no, the answer is no. You shouldn't care one bit if the guy is angry with you."

Rachel's words became slurred, "It's just that I know I'm a flirt. With this wine, I—I laid it on thick downstairs."

"You did, but flirting is one thing. Saying no to sex is something completely different. You should be able to flirt all you want. It doesn't give any man the right to expect something from you."

I heard them kiss, then Rachel asked, "Where the hell are my clothes?"

From the nook, I peeked around the corner and saw the pile of her clothes. If he retrieved the clothes and returned upstairs, I was safe. The clothes weren't the problem. The problem was that her shoes were by the pool table, in plain view.

His voice got louder when he responded, "They're right down here."

I glanced towards the bar across the room. There was no way I could make it over there. He was at the end of the hallway at the top of the stairs right above me.

Rachel raised her voice, "You don't have to get them. I just wondered where they were."

He stopped. "Are you sure?"

"I'm sure. I may need to eat another piece of pizza before you take me back to my car though."

"That's not good," Brent said.

"What?"

"Your foot is off the bed and on the floor. Is the room spinning?"

"Spinning is a little extreme," She spoke softer and half of normal speed, "but it is definitely rotating very slowly." She sighed heavily. "And it won't stop."

The house fell quiet for a moment, then Rachel slurred, "Doctor Brent Cooper, did you put something in my drink?"

I peeked around the corner. His shoes were near the pile of his clothes closer to the front door. I hid behind the wall again, then heard Dr. Cooper say, "Goodnight Rachel."

A door closed on the second floor that I guessed to be a bathroom. I ran up the stairs to the second floor and peered down the hallway towards the master bedroom. The doors were open, and Rachel was asleep or passed out with her foot on the floor. I ran across the living room and stuck the second camera to a dark lamp in the far corner that would give me a view of the full room and part of the hallway. Immediately, I ran up the next two sets of stairs to the third floor and stuck the third and last camera on and end table in the front corner by the theater. It faced toward the back door and part of the kitchen. A toilet flushed, and I hurried out the back door, got my rain gear from behind the hot tub and rushed down the wooden steps of the deck.

Inside the Branson house, I accessed the app to view the cameras I placed. There was no activity on any of them, so I viewed his security system.

SYSTEM: ARMED (STAY)

Rachel was still asleep in Dr. Cooper's bed, but Brent wasn't next to her. I thought, *Okay, so he's a gentlemanly, murderous lunatic.* I went through every camera on each floor. He didn't show up on any of them. Based on what I knew of his house, he was likely asleep in one of his "someday bedrooms," as he called them. I navigated to the camera in the master bedroom so I could act quickly if Rachel's status changed. I sat under the window and checked on her so frequently, it became an obsession. My heart would race. I clicked my fingernails together, bit my bottom lip and bounced my foot rapidly, but I couldn't stop until she moved or shifted. Both her feet were curled up under the white sheet. She laid on her side with her knees drawn to her chest.

A moment later, I saw the back of Dr. Cooper's head enter the frame. He casually walked to the edge of the pedestal and watched her. He was shirtless, with long dark pajama bottoms. I used my fingers to zoom in on my screen and moved the screen around until I could see each of his hands closely. Both were empty. I thought it was creepy that he stood at the end of the bed just to watch her sleep, then I thought of Katie playing softball at thirteen years old. She played shortstop and took a line drive to her forehead.

The batter swung. A loud crack echoed. The ball sped straight towards Katie at an estimated 83 mph. She held her glove in front of her face, but the ball came too fast, and her reaction time was too slow. The only reason it didn't kill her was that it grazed her glove before it hit her directly. Her arms and legs went limp. She fell backwards and her arms flopped on the ground. A synchronized gasp came from the bleachers. I ran around the fence to get to her. Her entire team surrounded her and screamed, "KATIE." The medic rushed out onto the field. When he cleared the team away, her teammates only moved back a few steps. I crouched down and tapped her shoulder, "Katie. Katie. KATIE!" I couldn't tell you a single detail about what the medic did. I just stared at my daughter's limp body. She didn't stop breathing, which was the only indication she was alive. Although it was only thirty seconds, it seemed like an eternity passed until she opened her eyes and held her forehead with her hand. When the paramedics readied the ambulance, and we got Katie on her feet, I shouted to Penny, "I'm going with her. I'll call you as soon as I know something."

The paramedics kept her alert and talking all the way to the hospital. The doctor confirmed she had a minor concussion. They monitored her for a few hours, then released her to go home.

I can't imagine the headache that followed. When she laid down that afternoon, I stood in her doorway. At times, I thought she was too quiet, so I walked to the edge of her bed and poked her shoulder with my finger just to get her to move, then hurried out her door. When I could tell she had settled from the hallway, I leaned on the door frame again.

There was a light knock at the back door. It was almost midnight. I went into the kitchen and stood by the back door.

"You in there, John?"

I opened the door for Todd and locked it when he came inside. He took his hat off and placed it on the counter next to the door, then shed his rain gear.

"Don't you ever sleep, Chief?"

"Probably about as much as you do. What's the word?"

"You might want to come in and have a seat."

I led him into the living room and peeked out the window, then checked the app. Dr. Cooper wasn't in view of the camera anymore. Todd stood in the middle of the room.

"John, what's going on?"

I didn't look away from the app, only held up a finger towards Chief Merritt. Rachel shifted again. I sighed and dropped my shoulders, then explained, "I've accessed his security system, so I have eyes everywhere in his house, but limited sound. His system is video surveillance only. I got in there earlier and placed one camera on each level with audio."

"And?"

"Unless we're dealing with divine intervention, the circumstances are far too incriminating to dismiss him."

"What do you have?" he asked.

"He's on a date."

"Where?"

"She's in his bed alone." I turned my phone around. "See?"

"Is she—"

"She's fine. Just drunk. I think he's sleeping in one of his spare rooms on the second floor."

"How does any of that incriminate him?"

Instead of answering his question, I asked my own. "What do you know about his past?"

"Other than his school records at U of W, his dad shot and killed his stepmom. His dad is still in prison. And he lived a couple of years with some neighbors that were close to the Coopers for a while."

"He shot her in self-defense," I told him.

"According to the records, she said he came after her and started hitting her, so she chased after him with an iron skillet. He fired his pistol, and she died at the hospital a couple hours later. He's locked up on a Murder 1."

"The events match, but the details don't based on what I heard."

"What do you mean?"

"She was an abusive drunk. Came after his dad with the skillet first. Split his head open. He pulled his pistol and shot her just before he passed out. They questioned the kid but blew him off. They assumed he just hated his stepmom, but that's not the worst of it."

"What is?" Chief asked.

"He told his date—"

"Does his date have a name?"

"Rachel. She never gave her last name. Anyway, he told Rachel that she had it coming to her. If his dad didn't kill her that night, Brent would have. It's not what he said, Chief. It's how he said it. He was so matter of fact, like he's still holding on to that night."

"Did he describe how he would have done it that night if his dad didn't?"

"No. The thing that bothers me the most is when a detective returned to the neighbor's house to tell him his stepmother was dead."

Chief listened intently, and I continued, "He laughed."

"Laughed?"

"Yes. He laughed and went to bed. Sounds quite proud of it, too. He tried to change the subject a few times, but when she came back to it, he had no problem continuing his story. It was like he was describing a movie he watched, not a traumatic event from when he was a kid."

Chief didn't interrupt. "Oh, when he asked about her last name, she said she didn't put it on the dating site because she never knows if a guy wants to take her out to dinner or is a murderous lunatic that wants to hack her up."

"How did he respond?"

"He said, 'If it's any consolation, Rachel, I'm not going to hack you up' like it was nothing. Then he mentioned something about stabbing her."

"What?"

"Not directly. She joked about she would rather he just tell her they can't date anymore instead of slicing and stabbing. He sounded like he was joking too, when he said he never told her anything about stabbing."

"Dammit." Todd raised his voice and pointed towards the back door. "Each of the girls I've pulled out of that fucking river were stabbed multiple times."

"Chief—"

"Don't fucking 'Chief' me! This son of a bitch is our guy. I knew it. I fucking knew it all along!"

"And you've got nothing," I stated firmly.

"What?"

"It's all circumstantial. You have no prints. You can't tie any of these victims to him."

"What the fuck do you know?"

"You wouldn't have called me if you did."

Todd shook his head, clenched his jaws together and said, "Goddammit." He stood toe to toe with me and pointed into my chest. "Tell me you can get this fucker. Tell me you're close enough to take him out if he does *anything* to her." He pointed towards the River House.

"I have audio. I have video. And I can disarm his security system. Jesus, I can go in there right now and sleep in one of his spare rooms if I want to, and he'd never know I was there."

Todd sighed. "There's not much time John. The river is rising at a pretty good rate. Most of it is from the rain to the North that started early yesterday."

"I pray there's *not* much time, Chief."

"What?"

"That's better than being too late."

Chief looked at the receiver, "What are those lights there?"

I spun to look. The lights for Microphone 3 got brighter, then dimmed as Microphone 2 activated. When they dimmed, Microphone 1 started flashing. Even standing in the middle of the room, we heard the loud scraping sound through the headphones.

Camera 1

The dark wall behind the bar wasn't a wall at all. There was light coming through it.

I quickly changed to Dr. Cooper's own security system. Rachel was still in bed, covered with a comforter. I enlarged the screen and stared.

"What's going on, John?"

I held up one finger but didn't take my eyes away from that screen. Chief Merritt stood next to me. I muttered, "Come on, Rachel. Move. Goddammit, please move."

"What did you see?" Todd asked.

I switched to my camera again. Todd pressed his shoulder against mine. "What the hell is that?"

I spoke slowly, "It's the wall behind his bar on the first floor. It's open."

"There's nothing on the other side of that wall, John. It's the end of the house."

"I know. He's not on the other side of the open wall."

"What do you mean? Where the fuck is he?"

I slowly looked into Todd's eyes. Stone-faced, I muttered, "He's under his house."

Chief Merritt's eyes opened wide. He patted me on my shoulder firmly, "Go, go, GO!!!"

I donned my rain gear quickly. Todd said, "Get the girl out of there."

"Chief. What the hell are you thinking? The man has a basement—maybe a tornado shelter. That's all we know."

Todd stood nose to nose with me and screamed, "I've had dead girls floating in my river for four years, John. Four fucking years!"

I screamed back, "And it's all circumstantial. Are you willing to risk your career on this?"

"You're goddamn right I am! But I'm not willing to risk the life of one more person."

"And what are you going to do when I've done your fucking dirty work and you get another floater, huh?"

He clenched his jaws together. His face twitched, and we stared into each other's eyes. Neither of us were willing to back down. I screamed again, "You willing to kill this man," I pointed towards the River House, "and find out the actual killer is still out there? What if it was your daughter?"

Todd screamed back, "What if it was yours, John?"

I struck him hard. He fell backwards and tripped over my backpack. I stood over him and pointed into his face and calmly said, "It *was* my daughter, you son of a bitch."

I walked out the back door and hurried under Dr. Cooper's deck. I shook with anger. It consumed me. I wasn't even certain I had everything I needed. I felt for my pistol around my back, then accessed his security system. The wall behind the bar was closed, so I checked every camera for Dr. Cooper. Rachel was still in his bed alone, and I didn't see Brent anywhere, not even through my own cameras.

The cameras I placed weren't completely useless. I pulled up Camera 1. There was no movement, but I put the speaker on the phone to my ear and listened with my eyes closed. After a full minute of silence, I changed to Camera 2. I watched for movement in the living room, kitchen, and end of the hallway so closely, I barely blinked. Seeing nothing, I held the speaker to my ear again. I heard faint snoring, so I accessed his master bedroom camera. Each of Rachel's breaths were deep and lifted the comforter several inches. The rhythm of her breathing matched the light snoring I heard through Camera 2. I activated Camera 3. Nothing.

Slowly, I crept up the wooden deck stairs. When I reached the second floor, I put my back to the wall and tried to look into the glass of the sliding door, but it was too dark to see. I went back to Camera 2 and watched the screen while I waved my hand slightly. There wasn't a delay, so I checked Dr. Cooper's third-floor camera that showed the back door. When I knew it was safe, I tiptoed to the third floor. Just as I reached for the door, I stopped and navigated to Dr. Cooper's security system and set it to SYSTEM: OFF (NOT RECOMMENDED).

I slowly turned the knob and opened the door just enough to squeeze inside, then closed it with the same level of caution.

When I saw him, it was already too late. The last thing I remember was a Dr. Cooper's arm raised up over his head. He brought it down fast, and I felt the needle enter the side of my neck.

Chapter 17

Prisoner

I felt like I was dreaming. I slowly regained consciousness but wasn't really awake. My body felt numb. It took all my strength just to open my eyes. I'd barely get them open, then they'd close again. They burned, like they would if something woke me from a deep sleep. It wasn't dark, but it wasn't light, either. Each brief moment I opened my eyes, I saw something. A light. I heard nothing. There was no ringing in my ears. It was complete silence, as if I were deaf, then I drifted again.

As I awoke the second time, I tried to move my head from side to side. I knew I was moving, but it felt like slow motion, even with my eyes still closed. My breathing was slow. I tried to lift my head. Somehow, I knew that the more I moved, the more whatever was in my body would dissipate. Why was there something in my body? My eyes opened again. Seeing a bit more clearly, I confirmed there was a light, but I didn't know where it came from. I lifted my head and could feel my eyes rolling around aimlessly. Then I remembered. A man stabbed me. With what, though? A knife? I felt around my stomach and my chest, then pulled my hand close to my face to inspect. I still couldn't focus, so I closed my eyes tightly and opened them rapidly. My ear drums shook from the effort to keep my eyes open. He stabbed me in the shoulder. No, my neck. My arm felt heavy when I lifted it to my neck and felt it, then put it in front of my face again.

My sense of hearing started to return. I heard white noise, like the hum of an air conditioner, but it still seemed like an echo. I yawned, and my hand flopped to my side. My eyes closed again, and I relaxed. I focused on my breathing. I *was* breathing—slow and steady. Shit, where was Dr. Cooper? Where the hell was I? My hearing returned completely. I opened my eyes again and kept them open longer, but still couldn't focus. The dream state faded. With my hand at my side, I cautiously felt underneath me. It wasn't smooth, but it was cold and hard, like concrete. I pressed my head downwards, but it didn't move. I was on the floor. But where? I opened my eyes wide a few times and turned my head to the left. My vision become somewhat normal again.

I was on a concrete floor with white cinderblock walls. It wasn't dirty. There was a single florescent light mounted in the ceiling. Is this a hospital? There were other lights. I didn't know how many, but none of the others were on. I turned my head farther. The wall was close, so I tried to sit up and lean my back on it, assuming that if I sat up, my mind would clear even more. The room was bigger than I first thought. There was a dark area beyond the florescent light. The room was spinning when I first leaned against the wall.

My head fell backwards against the cinderblocks. I kept moving my head and my arms, then stretched my ankles by pointing my toes straight, then back, then straight again. When the dizziness faded, I put my hands underneath me and stood. Just as I got to my feet, I heard a voice from the dark area of the room say, "I wouldn't do that if I were you?"

"Why not?" I asked defiantly.

As soon as I got to my feet and tried to take a step with my left foot, it stopped quickly and I crashed to the concrete floor again.

"Because I tied your feet together."

"Doctor Cooper?"

He didn't respond, but I was certain it was him.

"What did you do to me?"

He raised his voice, "I'm asking the fucking questions! What were you doing in my house?"

My cheek was on the cold concrete. The room spun again.

"I asked you a question. What were you doing in my house?"

"I just got back from the bar," I lied. "I thought it was my house."

"What's your name?"

I lifted my head to turn it towards him, then laid it flat on the concrete again.

He asked louder, "I said, What's your name?"

"I heard you, you prick."

I couldn't turn my face away completely before his leather boot landed on it. The cold concrete soothed my jaw for a moment before I felt the pain.

"Owe," I muttered.

I rolled over and leaned back against the wall. My jaw was throbbing. I pulled my bottom lip inside my mouth and tasted blood. My mouth watered. I looked down towards the floor and saw a string of red drool sway back and forth before it snapped.

I reached my right hand around to my back and felt my empty waistband.

Dr. Cooper asked, "You looking for this?" and waved my .45 back and forth.

I squinted and said, "Yep."

"You're lucky I didn't call the cops," he said. He laughed, then said, "Wait, no you're not. I get confused sometimes. I meant to say that you *would* be lucky *if* I called the cops—but I didn't."

In my semi-intoxicated state, I couldn't think of a wise-ass response quickly enough.

He asked again, "Now, let's start over since we've established that you're in a vulnerable state right now, shall we? What is your name?"

"My name is Brent—Brent Cooper," I lied again. "I'm a doctor. I was born in Portland, went to school in Seattle and settled here because I like small towns, seclusion, and the river."

I don't know how many times he hit me after that, but when I sat up again, I couldn't breathe through my nose and my vision was as blurry as when I regained consciousness.

"Why are you in my house?" he asked.

"Because you keep beating the shit out of me. I would have left by now if you didn't."

"You're below ground level, you know. The river's rising. It might flood in here."

He waited for a response that I never gave.

"Okay, so we're going to play like that."

I felt a needle in my neck again and passed out before I fell over.

When I woke up again, it was just like before. My eyes wouldn't open, I couldn't hear anything, and it took several minutes to shake it off. The only difference is when I woke up the second time, it was completely dark.

I sat against the wall again and pulled my hand in front of my face, but it was too dark to see. I didn't know what time it was. Hell, I didn't know what day it was. Was it still the middle of the night on Tuesday? I felt the floor. It was dry. The only thing I knew for sure was that he didn't knock me out long enough to heal from the beating. My entire face throbbed. When my head cleared completely, I crawled on the ground and rubbed my hands all around the floor to get my bearings. There wasn't much there. The only things I felt as I swiped back and forth, towards what used to be the dark area of the room, were the walls. I've always had a good sense of direction and was certain my serpentine sweep of the concrete floor was in the same direction. Based on the layout of his house and that he sat to my left when I awoke the first time, the stairs to the first floor had to be behind where he was sitting. When I reached the wall at the end, the only thing I felt against the concrete was more concrete.

I slowly stood and felt the walls. There had to be a door, or at least, a doorway to get to the stairs. From the left corner, I put my palms on the wall and pivoted my feet from my heels to my toes to move to my right. Somewhere between 12 and 15 feet away from the left corner, I felt the wooden door. I swiped my hands to the right, but it was flat, so I knew the doorknob was on the left. I put my hands directly to the knob, but there was nothing there. I pushed, but the door didn't budge. I sat on the ground in the right corner with my ear to the door but heard nothing. God, it was so dark. My heart raced, and I knew I needed to calm down, so I sat on the floor in the corner and relaxed the best I could. Just as I've said before, when I'm not busy, I only have time to think, and that's the worst thing I can do sometimes. My mind filled with what ifs. What if I don't get out of here? What if his next victim isn't a young pretty girl? How will I look when Chief Merritt pulls my decaying body from the river?

I imagined close-up photos of myself. My eyes were white. A ring of water perfectly framed my face. There were rocks under my head. The current near the amphitheater would try to pivot my feet downstream. The split in my lip would be much wider than it was at that moment. I pulled my hand up and touched several places around my face. My left eye would be swollen and almost shut. My nose would be wide. There's no doubt I'd have bruises all over my head. My feet were tied together and the flesh on my ankles around the zip tie would sway in the water like fish shit in an aquarium. Then I thought of Katie.

I thought of the first day of her Senior year. I thought of the night before, when she asked me what she should wear. The sweetest, but most painful memories flickered at thirty frames per second in reverse. I seemed to recall every hug. Every kiss on the cheek and every goddamn time she looked into my eyes and said, "I love you, Daddy."

I felt the tears in my eyes when I saw myself teach her how to ride a two-wheeler. She drew pictures for me. Every one of them had a big yellow sun with yellow rays coming off of it, dis-proportioned stick figures with enormous heads and huge hands on the ends of arms that didn't bend. There was always a crooked house balanced on tiny steps. She even made one of them into a dinner plate for me. I saw her as a toddler, wobbling with her arms up like a fucking orangutan when she took her first steps, then fell backwards on in her orange shorts. I whispered in the darkness, "I miss you so much, pumpkin butt."

We were in the delivery room. The doctor lifted her on display, all covered in blood and slime and shit, and announced, "It's a girl." She was the most beautiful thing I had ever seen in all my life. My friend. My princess. My daughter. I spent the last fourteen years searching for her killer. For absolution, for closure—for vengeance. Sitting on the cold concrete floor of that basement, for the first time, I questioned if I would ever have those things. I was cold. I was hungry. I was a prisoner.

I dropped, curled my feet up, wrapped my arms around my legs and buried my face. "I'm so sorry, Katherine."

I sobbed. My body shook. My shoulders jumped, and then I heard her voice. A distant echo, like a memory.

"Daddy."

I lifted my head and looked around in the darkness. I saw a light across from me, near the opposite wall.

"Baby?" I whispered.

"Daddy, it's me. It's Katie."

The light took shape. She looked radiant.

"Katie, sweetheart?"

"Yeah Daddy, it's me. Please don't cry for me. You're my safe place. My shelter. Today is not the day, Daddy. I miss you so much, but it's not time yet."

I reached out to her. She reached her hand to me, but I couldn't feel her. I wanted her to be real so badly. I wanted her to come back to me. I wanted the last fourteen years to be a terrible nightmare. I wanted to wake up and realize none of it really happened.

"It's not time yet, Daddy."

She faded, and I called out to her, "Katie?"

"It's not time yet."

She vanished, and I whimpered, "Not today, Katie. Not today."

I crawled all around the concrete floor and swiped my hands on every inch to find something. I didn't care what it was. There had to be something on the floor that I could use as a weapon. A pen. A nail. A fucking pine needle. I didn't care what it was, but I was going to find it and be ready for him when he came back down. I started along the edge of the floor with the door and kept going until I reached the far wall. When I did, I turned around and went back. I probably could have made wider paths, but I didn't want to take the chance that I would miss anything. As I got to each cinderblock wall, I straightened my back with my knees on the hard floor to feel the walls. Halfway back to where I started, I felt a protrusion from the wall no bigger than a large kernel of corn. I picked at it, but it was smooth. I used my thumbnail on each hand to crease it, then picked at it. I laid my hand flat on the wall again and felt the mortar lines of the masonry. The protrusion was nothing more than a buildup of mortar.

I kept swiping back and forth, even backtracked a little to be positive I missed nothing. I swiped furiously. I felt like I was panting; I was so out of breath. Then I felt something sticky. I lightened the pressure and felt with only my fingertips. I sat flat and made larger circles slowly with my hand. It was a puddle of something. The edges were sticky, but the middle was wet. I rubbed my fingers together, and they glided easily with the substance between them. I didn't know how far I had gone, so I crawled back to the corner by the door. My ankles burned from the zip ties cutting into my skin. When I reached the corner, I pivoted and felt my way back. I was in the same place that I woke up earlier. I touched my finger to the wet part in the middle of the puddle again and touched it to the tip of my tongue. Blood. My blood. I sat against the wall again, and leaned my head against the cinderblocks, defeated.

I opened my eyes wide when I heard something breathe in the darkness to my right. The breathing turned into a whimper, then deep sighs. I shifted slightly.

"Hello?" I heard a female's weak voice say.

"Is somebody there?" it said.

"Yes," I replied

She started crying, then screamed, "Let me go, you son of a bitch!"

"Miss be quiet," I demanded.

She cried harder, "Let me go, you bastard!"

"Miss—Miss—my name is John Wolfe. Doctor Cooper stabbed me with a needle, and I woke up down here."

"Can you tell me your name?"

"Where am I?" she cried.

"Miss, with all due respect, you need to shut the fuck up or you'll get us both killed."

Her cries turned back into whimpers.

I asked again, "Can you tell me your name?"

She took three deep breaths and whispered, "Barb. My name is Barb Collins."

Chapter 18

Time's Up

Out of habit, I reached for my phone from my belt clip. It didn't surprise me, it wasn't there.

"Barb, what has he done to you?"

She sniffled and said, "I can't feel my legs" in a normal tone.

"Barb, please keep your voice down. I'm going to get you out of here."

She whispered, "Are you the police?"

"No, just an agent sent to help."

"Do you work for the FBI?

"No—it doesn't matter."

She cried again. "I can't keep my eyes open."

"Are you hurt? What did he do to you?"

"I had surgery on my knee. When I woke up, I was angry and confused. I punched him."

I knew she couldn't see me in the dark, but the thought of anyone landing a good punch on Dr. Cooper brought a smile to my face.

She continued, "My husband took me home, then had to go to work. He works the night shift. I laid on the couch so I was close to everything I might need. I was sleeping and woke up to see Doctor Cooper standing above me. He stabbed me with a needle, and I woke up here."

"Is this the first time you've woken up?"

"No. My hands are tied behind my back. I asked him for some water. He told me I'd have plenty of water in the next few days, but he brought me a pitcher of water anyway. I sat up with my arms behind my back and he poured the entire pitcher into my mouth. I coughed, but he didn't stop pouring. He laughed and held my head so I couldn't pull away. He was going to drown me with a pitcher of water."

"What made him stop?" I asked.

"In the middle of hacking, I threw up on him and he hit me. He spoke so calmly when he said he wanted me to feel what it's like to drown, so I recognize it when it happens again. He said he wants me to feel the terror and know that I was going to die."

"Barb, were there lights on when he did that to you?"

"Just one over there, closer to the door.

"What's on the other side of you?"

"I don't know. It's so dark."

"Do you have any idea how big this room is past you?"

"I really don't know. Even if it was light enough, I'm not good at telling distance."

"You sound like you're higher than I am. Are you lying down or sitting up?"

"I'm on a cot of some sort. It feels like a hospital bed."

"Mrs. Collins, I'm going to push your bed over until you reach a wall. I want to know how far it is?"

"John, right?" she asked.

"Yes."

"Why does it matter?"

"I'm trying to find anything I can—anything at all to fight him."

"If there were sheets, I'd say that might work, but from what I could see, which wasn't much, there's nothing in here like that."

"I'm going to come over there, okay?"

"Okay."

I scooted on my butt to get to her. She was approximately ten feet away from me. Each time I moved, I winced.

"You're hurt. What did he do to you?"

"It doesn't matter, Mrs. Collins."

When I felt her bed, I laid flat on the ground and pushed it with my feet. The screeching sounds were loud and piercing.

"John, stop. He's going to come back."

"I have to try. I won't push as much this time."

I shifted closer and inched the bed away from me until it didn't move anymore.

"Barb, are you dressed?"

"What?"

"Are you dressed? Do you have clothes on? Shoes?"

"I'm wearing a t-shirt and sweatpants."

"What about shoes?"

"I still have my tennis shoes on because I thought it would support my knee better if I had to get up for—"

I interrupted her, "Tennis shoes, you say?"

"Yes."

"I can get us out."

"With my shoes?"

I got into a position where I could use Barb's bed to help me stand.

"I need to get to your shoelaces. I'll feel around the bed until I get to them, okay?"

"Okay."

When I stood, I felt her bed in the darkness until I got to her shoes, untied one of them, removed the shoelace, then sat against the wall again. I wrapped the shoelace through the zip tie around my ankle and used it like a saw.

"John, what are you doing?"

"I'm going to cut through the ties on my ankles with your shoelace."

I kept cutting. It took a lot of pressure to cause the friction necessary to cut through. The more pressure I used, the more the ties cut into my flesh. Lighter pressure wouldn't get it done. I took a deep breath, gritted my teeth, and pulled hard on one end at a time as fast as I could. The pain was so intense, I'd rather get my ass kicked by Dr. Cooper ten more times than finish cutting through that zip tie.

"Did you get it?" she asked.

My only response was grunts and muffled groans. I stopped for a moment and didn't know how close I was to cutting through. I took a few deep breaths but kept some pressure on the shoelace so it didn't move along the zip tie, which would have made me start over. With one more deep breath, and as much pressure as I could, I cut as hard and fast as possible. I was about to scream when my torso flew backwards and hit the wall. It broke free. I took several deep breaths and finally answered, "I got it."

"Barb, do you have a phone or anything in your pockets?"

"No."

I put my hands in front of me and limped towards the door and listened with the shoelace in my hand. The pain in my ankles was intense. I sat down when there was no sound on the other side. Mrs. Collins fell asleep again. I could tell by the way she breathed. I wondered where the hell he was. I had no concept of time. Had hours passed, or merely minutes between standing up, walking around and sitting back down to rest my ankles? Mrs. Collins woke up a few times, then fell back asleep. Sometimes, while she was awake, she'd ask if I was still there, then she'd cry.

I put the shoelace in my pocket and walked to the back wall and felt the floor around from the corner where Barb was and inched to the left. There was a break in the wall. I felt around where the break was. It was smooth, like glass. I rubbed my palms all around the glass. It was cold. Was it a window? A door? I rubbed my fingers along the edges, then across every inch from top to bottom.

There was a lip of concrete below the glass, but nothing on the glass itself. I pushed in and tried to push it to the left, then to the right, but it didn't move. I kept feeling along the wall on the other side of the glass. There was more cinderblock wall, but only the width of two blocks. As I dragged my hand down the block wall, I felt something round. I pushed it. A loud, but muffled motor started. It had to have run for a minute or more. There was another muffled noise from the other side of the glass. When it stopped, I heard air release loudly, and the glass opened towards me. I stepped over the concrete lip, like stepping into a shower. I stepped into water that covered my shoes, but not up to my ankles. The river rose, and the flood was ebbing into his basement. There was cinderblock on each side of me. I stepped farther in and there was another cold glass wall.

The light in the basement turned on. Instinctively, I turned around, took the shoelace out of my pocket and ran to the corner by the door. I heard him on the other side, shouting, "What the fuck is going on down here?"

With my back pressed as far into the corner as possible, the basement door hinged towards me. I held each end of the shoestring in my hands and raised it just above my head. When Dr. Cooper stepped through, I quickly put the shoestring around his neck and pulled as tightly as I could.

Mrs. Collins woke up and screamed. Brent grasped at his neck and thrashed around, but the choker was too tight for him to get his fingers between the shoestring and his neck. He tried to scream, but only raspy choking sounds echoed through the basement. I had never choked someone before, and it was taking much longer than I thought it would. He put up a good fight. I shifted around like a parasite on his back and kept pulling the string tighter.

He stopped moving his feet, but still thrashed his torso. He lifted his left foot and kicked my leg. His boot slid down my shin and peeled the skin back from my ankle. I screamed but didn't loosen my grip. He fell silent, and his thrashing slowed. He stopped moving his feet and swayed. His fight faded, and he dropped one knee to the ground. I kept pulling. His other knee met the ground, and I put mine into his back. He put his arms in front of him and leaned forward. I pulled as hard as I could and pushed him forward with my knee. The shoestring snapped in half and he fell flat on the concrete.

Mrs. Collins screamed. I ran to her and said, "Come on, we have to get out of here."

"John, I can't move my legs."

"I'll come back for you."

She grabbed my arm, "Don't leave me here."

"Barb, I'm going to get help. I'll be right back. I swear to you, I won't be gone more than five minutes."

"John, please."

I slowed down and said calmly, "There's another girl. She's in the house upstairs. I need to check on her, then I promise, I'll be—right—back."

She shook her head with tears falling down her face, but I knew she understood when she released my arm. She looked at Dr. Cooper's dead body on the cold concrete floor and whispered, "Hurry."

I took her hand in both of mine and said, "I will."

I hurried up the stairs in pain. What time was it? What day was it? Where was my pistol and phone? Above all, is Rachel okay?

At the top of the stairs, I pulled the wall open with the handle, which made a loud scraping sound. The same I heard Tuesday afternoon when Brent got home from work. I limped but hurried across the game room. The piles of clothes weren't there. There was light through the glass of the front door. It was daytime. My mind raced as I put together the details.

He came home late in the Tacoma with the covered bed. I had forgotten to arm his security system. I thought it was too late to arm it, but it wasn't. Once I armed the system, I couldn't figure out why it took him so long to get into the house. He was retrieving Mrs. Collins from the bed of his truck. Why didn't I see it? I watched the cameras. Were they my cameras or his? I realized they were his. I didn't set my own until he was in the house with Rachel. But I wasn't watching his cameras. When he disarmed the security system, he didn't set it to STAY. He turned it off, so the cameras weren't active. He brought Mrs. Collins into the game room, opened a beer from the cooler behind the bar and left the cap upside down on the top. That's when I heard the wall open for the first time. It was loud, and it startled me, so I threw the headphones into my lap. He closed the wall while the headphones rested on my legs. Twenty minutes passed without the microphones activating. That's when he was in the basement with Mrs. Collins.

I went to the second floor and into the master bedroom. The bed was made and there was no sign of Rachel, so I limped up to the third floor. The kitchen counters were empty. The table they sat around on the deck was empty. It was still raining. Where the hell is my phone? I returned to the second floor and went into the kitchen. On the other side of the refrigerator, my phone and .45 were on the counter next to Brent's phone. Next to my phone was a fifteen-

foot cable for a dog. I pushed a button on his phone and read the message on
his locked screen.

RACHEL

7:50 AM

LOL. Yeah, no kidding there. And Yes,
I'd love to see you tomorrow night
after work. And yes, you can take me
anywhere you want. I'm still okay with
hanging out at your place again. We
never did play those games.

I put his phone in my back pocket, my .45 in the waist of my jeans then
unlocked my phone.

FULLER

WEDNESDAY 10:50 PM

Where are you, John? Don't you like
my little game? You can't hide from
me forever.

I stared at my phone for a moment, then closed my eyes and thought of the
smile on Katie's face. She was the only reason I was alive. And I couldn't
remember a single day of my life that I felt *more* alive. My current mission
was complete. The delay was over. I'd be on the road within hours. Then I
imagined wrapping a shoestring around Fuller's neck and pulling tightly. But

that wasn't good enough. That wasn't near good enough. I wanted to see his face. I wanted to watch the life fade from his eyes. I sent one message.

FULLER

THURSDAY 8:40 AM

Time's up.

The pain in my left shoulder came at the same time as I heard the gun shot from behind me.

Chapter 19

The Last Victim

I dropped to my knees, then slowly turned around.

Dr. Cooper stood at the top of the steps. He coughed once, then lowered his pistol. I reached around my back for my own. He fired again. The bullet grazed my hand. I lifted my hand in front of me. It shook and blood ran down the edge of my palm opposite my thumb. I put my hands up and whispered, "At least let me face you. I don't want to die with my back turned."

He hurried past me and got the dog's lead from the counter and connected the end around the cable, so it looped around my neck. He pulled the lead. I took a deep breath, an instant before it tightened around my throat and he started walking down the stairs. I walked on my knees to keep up and tried to stand but ran out of floor before I could. He jerked the cable and my body tumbled down the stairs. I felt the pistol fall out of my waistband as I bounced from stair to stair. The speed of my fall caused the tension on the cable to loosen, and I took a few breaths before I hit the bottom. I got one foot flat on the floor before my head jerked forward again and he dragged me across the game room. I grabbed the lead with both hands to release the tension just enough to take another breath. When he felt the cable tug my direction, he turned around and kicked me in the face again.

While on the ground, I heard distant sirens. He stayed still and looked around aimlessly with wide eyes. The front door burst open. A shot fired. Brent's chest oozed blood instantly, and he dropped to the ground. I quickly removed the lead from around my neck and looked behind me. Chief Merritt stood in the doorway with his pistol still aimed. He fired again. I turned in time to see more blood burst out of Dr. Cooper's chest. He fell backwards. I stood and retrieved the .45 from the second to last step, then limped towards him. Todd lowered his pistol and joined me. Neither of us spoke. I held my right hand above my heart to slow the bleeding, then pointed my pistol at Dr. Cooper's chest with my left hand and fired. Chief Merritt fired. Both of us kept shooting until the bolts on our pistols locked backwards. I pulled my trigger again, just to be sure.

I dropped my head, then coughed several times.

Chief Merritt asked, "You okay?"

"Yeah."

I looked into his eyes and said, "Thanks."

We both looked at Dr. Cooper's body. I asked Todd, "How did you know?"

"I didn't. One of my officers—Matthews was in a boat. We have another body."

I shook my head, "No—that can't be." I looked at Dr. Cooper again. "That's impossible."

"It's possible. She just surfaced twenty minutes ago. Why is it impossible?"

"He was in the basement twenty minutes ago. I choked him. Goddamn."

I couldn't believe what he told me. "Did he find her at the amphitheater again?"

"No. When he first saw her, she was floating from under Doctor Cooper's dock."

I tilted my head back and shook it with my eyes closed, "No, no—no!"

"What is it, John?

"You better come with me," I told him.

Todd's cell phone rang. "Yeah," he answered. A few seconds later he responded, "I'll be right there."

"You're going to have to give me the tour another time. Matthews found a drain under Doctor Cooper's dock."

"I know what's on the other side of the drain, Chief."

"What is it?"

"Come with me."

I walked towards the open wall. Todd followed.

"Oh, there's another woman down there," I said.

"What? Who?"

"Her name is Barb Collins. She was one of Brent's patients."

"Jesus."

He made a phone call and said, "I need to compare the names of all victims to patients of Doctor Brent Cooper. Check them all, but right now, I'm looking specifically for a Barbara Collins." He paused, "Yes, Barbara Collins."

He ended the call and I led him to the basement. Just before I walked through the door, I called out, "Mrs. Collins, it's John. It's over. I have an officer with me."

There was a panel of light switches next to the door and a button, like the one by the glass door in the basement. I turned on all the switches. Mrs. Collins wept and said, "Oh, thank God," when she saw Chief Merritt.

Todd walked across the basement and his mouth gaped open, "Jesus Christ," he muttered.

On the far wall of the basement was a glass door. There were lights inside the small room on the other side. We walked up to the glass. On the other side of the small room, there was another glass door covered entirely with water.

Todd asked, "What the hell is this?"

I remembered the sounds I heard when I pushed the button next to the door, then walked back to the panel outside the basement. I held my hand over the button and looked through the basement when I pushed it.

The second piece of glass opened, and the small room filled with river water. When it filled, I walked next to Chief Merritt. He stared in awe, then looked at me slowly. I reached for the button on the thin cinderblock wall next to the hatch and pushed it. The second door closed, then a pump ran loudly. The level of the river water that filled the little room lowered until there were only a few inches of water in the bottom, then the door in front of us opened.

I put my hand on Todd's shoulder and said, "I felt this button twenty minutes ago in the dark and pushed it."

We both stared into the small room with the tunnel filled with river water on the other side of the second glass door.

"I released the body," I said.

Todd covered his mouth and shook his head. "Who was it?"

"I don't know. It was dark. I was trying to find a way out."

The phone in my back pocket vibrated.

RACHEL

Any chance I can call you? I just want
to hear your voice.

"It's the girl," I said.

Todd held his hand out and I handed him the phone. He tried to unlock it by entering generic passcodes. The first one he tried was 1, 2, 3, 4. He muttered, "Fucking idiot," when the phone unlocked.

He found Rachel in Dr. Cooper's call history and called.

She answered softly, "Hi there. Sorry if I'm bothering you. I just can't stop thinking about you."

"Ma'am, this is Chief Todd Merritt of the Mount Placid Police Department."

She was silent.

"Ma'am?"

"Yes, I'm here. What happened to Brent? Is he okay?"

"If it's not too much of a bother, can you come down here?"

"To the police department?"

"No ma'am, to Mister Cooper's residence."

"Why? What's going on?"

"I'll explain when you get here."

"Uh—yeah, um—I can be there in—" she sighed, "ten minutes—maybe fifteen."

"That's fine, Ma'am."

He ended the call and approached Mrs. Collins. "You okay?"

She sobbed.

Chief pushed the button on his walkie-talkie, "1101 to dispatch."

A female's voice responded, "Dispatch"

"I need a 10-48 at the end of Rivers Edge Lane."

"Copy. 10-48 at the end of Rivers Edge Lane."

"10-4," he said, then told Barb, "We're going to get you out of here."

Through tears, she asked Todd, "May I please call my husband?"

He unlocked his cell phone for her and she called, but couldn't talk when her husband answered. She nodded a few times, and whimpered, "Yeah, I'm okay."

I followed Todd upstairs, and we walked outside to the dock. One of the officers took one look at me and said, "Jesus Christ." He went to his car and put a first-aid kit on his hood. I held my hand above my heart while he opened the roll of gauze and a bandage.

Raven barked loudly. The rain was light. There were police cars everywhere and officers milled around. There was a blue tarp set up near the dock that was nearly level. The river raged. One officer took several photos of the dead woman on the bank.

"I want to see her," I said to Todd.

He started rebutting, but stopped, "John, I can't—" He looked at the girl, then at me. "Come on."

My hand was wrapped like a fighter's and he put a butterfly bandage by my left eye. When he finished, I walked with Todd.

Her eyes were white. She had a line around her neck where she was strangled. Blood stained her shirt, and her skin was partly decomposed.

I asked, "What's her name?"

Todd said, "We don't know yet."

"I want to know. Whenever you find out. Will you tell me her name?"

Todd nodded, then turned to look along Rivers Edge. A Corolla was bouncing along the pitted road and slid to a stop on the gravel in front of Brent's house.

Rachel jumped out quickly and started running towards the front door, "What's going on? Where's Brent?"

Todd hurried towards her, "Miss? MISS!!!" he shouted, but she entered the open door before he could stop her. She screamed.

"Miss, you need to come with me."

"NO! What did you do to him?"

I called her name, "Rachel."

She turned to me. "How do you know my name?"

"Please, come out here, and I'll explain everything."

She knelt by his dead body and sobbed.

I reached for her arm and said, "Please. Come with me and I'll explain. He's not the man you think he was."

Her body shook, but she let me help her up. I tried to turn her away, but she only backed up and didn't look away from him.

"Rachel, come on. Please come with me."

I held each of her shoulders and walked beside her to guide her out of the house to Chief Merritt.

"I'm Todd Merritt. I called you down here."

He removed his raincoat and wrapped it around Rachel. She looked towards the dock. "Who is that? What the hell is going on?"

The ambulance eased along Rivers Edge with lights on, but no sirens. Raven kept barking from inside her doghouse. Ted Johnson was on his porch. Todd shouted, "Sir, can you please take your dog inside?"

Ted shouted back, "Why don't you tell me what the hell is going on?"

"Sir, please. Just take your fucking dog inside."

He walked to the doghouse, released Raven from her lead and walked her inside by her collar.

The paramedics exited the ambulance and wheeled a gurney towards the front door. Todd said, "Inside the front door to the right. At the end of the room, there's a set of stairs, she's down there." Rachel leaned on his police car. Todd told her, "Stay right here. I'll be right back."

He ran to the paramedics. "There's a body on the floor to the right. Stay to the left of the room."

I unlocked my satellite phone and sent a message to Sam.

Subject Terminated

I've monitored your condition from
here through your smart watch. How
are you?

I've been better.

What happened?

I sent a summary of the events since Tuesday morning. Then sent one final message.

I'm taking that leave now. I'll report
when I'm available again.

Todd called my name. When I approached him, he said, "There's no record of Barbara Collins as one of Doctor Cooper's patients."

"How can that be?" I asked.

"He's changing their names in the computer network. I'm going to request surveillance from inside the hospital to confirm. Come with me, please."

He led me to Rachel.

"Miss, tell me about your relationship with Mister Cooper."

"We're dating," she said.

"He's your boyfriend?"

"We're not there yet. Only been on two dates."

"When was the last time you saw him?"

"Tuesday night. Well, yesterday morning when he took me to my car."

"Tell me every detail you can remember from the time you saw him Tuesday until you left yesterday morning."

Rachel described the date in the same detail as I observed. When she finished, she asked, "Chief Merritt, what's going on? How does all of this concern me and Brent?"

"You're aware of the bodies recovered from the Placid River, near the amphitheater, right?"

"No, I don't watch the news." She looked toward the dock. Tears welled in her eyes. She looked at the front door and covered her mouth. She shook again, "No. It can't be. He's such a gentleman. He wouldn't do that."

Todd took a deep breath and dropped his head for a moment, then looked at Rachel again. "Oh, my God. You really think—"

I said, "We don't think—we know, Rachel. I'm sorry."

"What happened to you?" she asked me.

I pointed towards the front door and she covered her mouth again.

"You're lucky to be alive, ma'am," I said. "There's one detail you're not thinking about."

She looked into my eyes and I began, "Tuesday night. You were on the porch on the third floor."

"Yes."

"I was under the deck and heard the entire conversation. I want you to think about what happened to his parents. Think about how he reacted when the detective returned to his neighbor's house and told him his stepmom was— had passed away."

Her eyes widened.

"You remember what he told you? What he would have done if his father didn't?"

Her stomach tightened and her body jerked forward. She ran to the front of the police car, supported herself with one hand on the hood and threw up.

I touched Todd's shoulder, "You got this?"

"Yeah."

I offered him my hand, "Thank you," I said sincerely.

"Where are you going?"

"I have another case I need to get on."

"Not before the paramedics tend to you."

"Chief, I'm fine."

"Do me a favor before you go, will you?"

"Sure. Anything."

He stepped towards the door to his car and pointed at the driver's side mirror. "Take a look."

I did as he said. My lips were split in multiple places. The left side of my mouth looked like a terrible injection job. My eye was cut and still wet with blood around the bandage.

Todd continued, "You've been limping since I saw you. What happened?"

I pulled up the legs of my jeans.

"Fuck. What the hell did he do to you?"

"I sort of did it to myself. He tied my ankles with zip ties and I crawled around the floor."

"That was smart," he said with obvious sarcasm.

I smiled, "I'm alive, aren't I?"

He shook his head and said calmly, "Go sit the fuck down."

"Yessir. Where would you like me to go, sir?"

"How about on the back of the ambulance, you hard-headed son of a bitch?"

I laughed, then hobbled to the ambulance.

The paramedics brought Barb out on the gurney. She asked them to stop next to me.

"Thank you, John. I owe you my life," she said.

I nodded.

Another officer approached Todd with a pocket-sized notebook, "Chief," he started. He looked down but glanced to me discretely.

Todd responded, "Yes," then noticed the officer flip his notebook open. "What do you have?"

"We have a name on the victim."

Todd put his hand on my shoulder. I winced. "Shit. I'm sorry man." His hands waved around while he tried to decide what to do with them. He sighed and said, "Don't go anywhere. I'll be right back."

He tipped his hat to me, then followed the other officer to the river.

My phone vibrated.

SAM

You've exposed the agency. You're
fired.

Chapter 20

Let the Fun Begin

Virginia Geist. That was the girl's name who I unknowingly released into the raging river by pushing the button on the wall in Dr. Cooper's basement. According to Chief Merritt, she died sometime between Sunday night and Monday morning.

She was a nineteen-year-old runaway prostitute who worked the alley off Second Street in the town center. The MPPD worked diligently to find out where she came from. Where was her family? They searched Missing Persons database but didn't find a match.

My opinion is neutral as far as the prostitution ring. I don't know enough to feel strongly either way. Some say they're social outcasts and officials shouldn't spend time looking for them when they're missing. Todd feels quite strongly that they're victims themselves. Mount Placid had a lucrative prostitution ring. When Todd has interviewed them, they've given several reasons for entering the industry. For some, it starts with hard drugs made in back street garage labs by kids who were too dumb to pass Science class but think they're smart enough to alter their product with crazy shit, to make theirs better than the next dumb ass. Some of the most addictive drugs are also the most affordable. One hit, one needle, one time—that's all it takes sometimes. First, they get addicted to the feeling. The escape from reality. It's an easy way to run away without ever moving their feet. They want more. One poor decision can lead to a worse situation. Some were robbed while they were on their 30-gauge vacation. Some just want more.

If you think for a second, these things are hard to find on the streets, bring your golden ticket and I'll take you down the rabbit hole to see meddlesome fairies, sparkling unicorns and tail-thrashing dragons. It's just past the second star to the North and on until morning.

When the addict comes back from vacation, they're similar to you and me. Shit sucks and we wish we never left. The only difference is they buy more. When they run out of money, they think no respectable employer will hire them in their current state. That's the moment options they never considered before become viable. They're attractive and realize they have a previously unrealized asset people want and are willing to pay for. As scary as it might be the first time, once it's been done, it gets easier.

According to Chief Merritt, some enter through the trafficking industry. In all cases, Todd treats them as victims, not social outcasts. He will never turn his eyes away from a prostitute who wants out. The human business in Mount Placid isn't as bad as some places. Chief believes he can shut it down within six months. He's partnered with some of the local politicians in a campaign to help them get straight, and to utilize skills they already have to make a decent wage so they can transition out of the industry. When I asked him if that's the same as transitioning back into society, he made it clear that they're part of society already. If they weren't, prostitution wouldn't exist. The ugly truth is as long as the industry has customers, it will remain prosperous. That's why he feels so strongly that it's not about transitioning them into society, but rather out of the industry.

The vast unknown is, where did Virginia Geist come from? Why did she run away? Why did she choose Mount Placid? The only thought that keeps running through my mind is why me? Why did our paths cross? For fuck's sake, why the Hell didn't I take action against Dr. Cooper sooner than I did. I was there. Possibly, right across the fucking river while she was still alive.

Jesus. Nineteen-years-old. As harsh as this might sound, life is a series of choices. Infants don't understand choices. They only understand reward and punishment. They do something, then get their hand smacked, or a scolding finger pointed at them. After a while, they start to learn when they do a thing, a bad thing happens, so they learn not to do that thing. When they do a thing and are rewarded, they do that thing again and again. At the core of human decisions is that people repeat behaviors that benefit them and stop behaviors that punish them. Sometimes, the benefit is that they feel powerful. They enjoy the feeling they get when they torture another. Most know it's wrong, some don't, but most do. The ones that know it's wrong and repeat the behavior is because they haven't been punished enough for that behavior. People make their own choices. In every choice, there is a consequence. How the consequence is perceived is what makes a person either repeat the behavior or stop it.

Virginia Geist liked to be paid for sex. Dr. Cooper liked killing people. Sunday night, coincidence met opportunity. If Virginia didn't know the risk, it was her own damn fault. If Dr. Cooper thought he'd never get caught, it was his. I didn't move in on the River House until it was too late. A failure of imagination. Objects in the rear-view mirror sometimes are incredibly clear. That's why he was gone Sunday night and why I couldn't see him on his cameras when he was home Monday morning.

Sunday night, he lured her. Monday morning, he tortured her in his basement. When the river rose enough, he put her in that goddamn sealed chamber. If I moved quickly enough, I could have saved her life, and saved Mrs. Collins a lot of mental anguish.

You know what? Fuck it. I can't change that. The girl is dead. Maybe because I failed. Maybe because of the choices *she* made. If it was because of her own choices, may God have mercy on her soul. If it was because of my failure, may God have mercy on mine. I don't believe in ghosts, but if I did, and she's dead because of me, that girl is going to haunt my ass for a very long time.

Rachel stuck around long enough to answer more of Chief Merritt's questions, then left the scene. Maybe I'll see her around Mount Placid sometime. I don't envy her. Monday night, she went to dinner with a man who kidnapped a woman and put her in his basement an hour before. The same basement Virginia was in. Both were directly underneath Rachel while she was in the game room, oblivious. It could have ended much worse for Rachel.

Why do I hear Dr. Cooper mocking his father again? *Work for what you need, pray for what you want and never wish for something different.* I guess it's like the butterfly effect, Rachel didn't know the alternative and neither do I.

Hell, I don't know much, but I *do* know this—there was nothing I wanted more than for this case to be over so I could move on to the next. That's exactly what I faced and there was nothing else in my way.

Todd made me promise that I would go home to heal before I go to Indy. How quickly things happen. Three days ago, on Thursday, I killed Dr. Brent Cooper. The Thursday before, I was on a ridge above the Mountainview Motel. Curtis, the innkeeper, scouted the field behind the Motel for a place to bury the bodies of victims that hadn't even checked in yet. Friday, just after midnight, two other guests checked in. Curtis nearly shot one of them. By daylight, the mission was over, and I was on my way to the midway, but stopped for breakfast before I checked in.

Why did you do it, Detective? Why did you take me out there on Halloween night? Why did you introduce me to the agency?
Because it's fun. Now all you have to do is find me.

I would find him soon enough. I had plenty of time to consider how I would do it. Trust me, there's no failure of imagination there. Many options were already on the table. And I had hours to imagine more.

Which method would I get the greatest perceived benefit? I was never much for creativity in my life. I wasn't good in art class. Katie used to ask me to help her with crafts, and everything I touched seemed to fall apart. My military experience conditioned me to think rationally, not creatively.

Sometimes we find ourselves in unexpected situations every day and respond to them accordingly. Events rarely play out the way we think they will in our minds. From sending my daughter off to her Senior year, to the message I received Thursday sitting on the back of the ambulance. We plan. I guess planning is a form of creativity itself. No reason to stress over situations that were out of our control. Creative or not, I've had fourteen years of thinking of the most heinous ways to murder my daughter's killer. I couldn't wait for the opportunity. Regardless of the situation I'm presented with, I had an answer. I had a method. I thought of Katie. I looked up to the sky as my lip tightened. *It's almost over, Pumpkin Butt. I love you so much.*

In a few hours, I'll be on my way to Indianapolis. I'm finally going after Fuller, with or without the protection of the agency. God, this is going to be fun.

Case

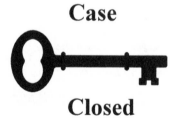

Closed

Acknowledgements

Thanks to my advanced readers, Cassie Alford, Mel Brown, Gracie Coons, Maryann Krajewski, Lindsay Metternich, Steve Miles, and Marti Sholty.

This book challenged me in many ways. From the details of early chapters to several months of writer's block. That's absolutely a real thing. I use a method that I learned from Stephen King's, *On Writing: A Memoir of the Craft* called situational writing. I didn't create an outline. I didn't make a flow chart with scenes. I just wrote. I put John Wolfe and other characters in situations and based on character development in the book and in my head, I wrote. I didn't know how they would get out of the situations and there were times I backed myself into a corner. Dr. Cooper was innocent. Dr. Cooper was the killer. Maybe the negative neighbor Ted was guilty. The ending was as much a surprise to me as it was to you. When I started the book, Dr. Cooper was supposed to kill Rachel. He wanted to, but he didn't expect he was going to like her as much as he did. I grew fond of Rachel, too so I couldn't kill her. I added so many twists, that I didn't know where the story would go from the end of any given chapter and almost gave up. I reflected on if crime thrillers should be a form of entertainment for people when real world victims were never entertained.

I want to thank several people who believe in my writing. Starting with Kris who encouraged me with every word I wrote. Dad, who only reads non-fiction, but still supports my work. I'll add a few people that I met over the last year who encouraged without knowing it. Steve Miles told a room full of people that someday, the world will know my name because, "his writing is *that* good." Joel Myers was the first to add a link to my website to his own and regularly says, "Just keep writing, buddy."

Thank you to the fans on social media who react to my posts with enthusiasm. God willing, I will keep writing and give my best to every publication. To all of you who took the time to read this book: Thank you!

About the Author

Pete Nunweiler is an emerging multi-genre author whose talent includes motivational self-development, a memoir and fiction. He has the keen ability to capture emotion in his writing through relatable characters and experiences.

One of the most unique tidbits about Pete's writing is that all of his books tie together somehow. When writing his memoir, One Hundred Seventy Days, he practiced the 5 Waters of Success that he teaches in How Much Water Do We Have?: 5 Success Principles to Conquer Any Challenge and Thrive in Times of Change. In his fiction series, The Ghost Between Us, the first four chapters have been described as very emotional and are based on his experiences from his memoir. Characters in The Ghost Between Us stay in Room 22, next to the room John Wolfe is watching in Room 23. In an upcoming paranormal horror, Virtual Assistant, look for characters in previous books.

Visit him at www.petenunweiler.com and sign up for email alerts to stay informed of upcoming releases and updates.

Other Books by Pete Nunweiler

Room 23 – Book one of the John Wolfe Series

The Ghost Between Us - A paranormal trilogy

One Hundred Seventy Days – A Caregiver's Memoir of Cancer and Necrotizing Fasciitis.

A mother is taken to the emergency room where she's seen by a doctor for the first time in forty-two years. What started as a simple procedure has escalated into a deadly situation. Her strength and her family's bond are tested when she is taken into one surgery after another. As her medical representative, the youngest son is faced with making crucial decisions that will determine her survival. When he receives the shocking news of the existence of a tumor, his options become extremely limited and the family is thrust into an emotional roller coaster.

One Hundred Seventy Days is the powerful true story of the unwavering strength of a woman and the indivisible bond of her family.

How Much Water Do We Have?: 5 Success Principles for Conquering any Challenge and Thriving in Times of Change

Do you have the 5 waters of success? Information, Planning, Motivation, Support, and Leadership. These essential elements will empower you to conquer any challenge and thrive in times of change. **How Much Water Do We Have?** *equips you to recognize the signs of dehydration at work and at home. You'll learn how to find, acquire, and use the 5 Waters of Success – and how to share them with your team and family members. Are you thirsty? Dive in!*

@5WatersBook, #5Waters

Published by Dave Burgess Consulting, Inc.

Coming Soon

Vitrual Assistant: A paranormal horror

CPSIA information can be obtained
at www.ICGtesting.com
Printed in the USA
LVHW010611201021
700907LV00004B/17